The Ship of ADVENTURE

Enid Blyton, who died in 1968, is one of the most successful children's authors of all time. She wrote over seven hundred books, which have been translated into more than forty languages and have sold more than 400 million copies around the world. Enid Blyton's stories of magic, adventure and friendship continue to enchant children the world over. Her beloved works include The Famous Five, Malory Towers, The Faraway Tree and the Adventure series.

Titles in the Adventure series

The
Ship of
ADVENTURE

Enid Blyton

MACMILLAN CHILDREN'S BOOKS

First published 1950 by Macmillan Children's Books

This edition published 2014 by Macmillan Children's Books
a division of Macmillan Publishers Limited
20 New Wharf Road, London N1 9RR
Basingstoke and Oxford
Associated companies throughout the world
www.panmacmillan.com

ISBN 978-1-4472-6280-0

1 3 5 7 9 8 6 4 2

A CIP catalogue record for this book is available from the British Library.

Typeset by Intype Libra Ltd
Printed and bound by CPI Group (UK) Ltd, Croydon CR0 4YY

Contents

1

A grand holiday plan

'Mother's got something up her sleeve,' said Philip Mannering. 'I know she has. She's gone all mysterious.'

'Yes,' said his sister, Dinah. 'And whenever I ask what we're going to do these hols she just says "Wait and see!" As if we were about ten years old!'

'Where's Jack?' said Philip. 'We'll see if he knows what's up with Mother.'

'He's gone out with Lucy-Ann,' said Dinah. 'Ah – I can hear old Kiki screeching. They're coming!'

Jack and Lucy-Ann Trent came in together, looking very much alike with their red hair, green eyes and dozens of freckles. Jack grinned.

'Hallo! You ought to have been with us just now. A dog barked at Kiki, and she sat on a fence and mewed like a cat at him. You never saw such a surprised dog in your life!'

'He put his tail down and ran for his life,' said Lucy-Ann, scratching Kiki on the head. The parrot began to

1

mew again, knowing that the children were talking about her. Then she hissed and spat like an angry cat. The children laughed.

'If you'd done that to the dog he'd have died of astonishment,' said Jack. 'Good old Kiki. Nobody can be dull when you're about.'

Kiki began to sway herself from side to side, and made a crooning noise. Then she went off into one of her tremendous cackles.

'Now you're showing off,' said Philip. 'Don't let's take any notice of her. She'll get noisy and Mother will come rushing in.'

'That reminds me – what's Mother gone all mysterious about?' said Dinah. 'Lucy-Ann, haven't you noticed it?'

'Well – Aunt Alison *does* act rather as if she's got something up her sleeve,' said Lucy-Ann, considering the matter. 'Rather like she does before somebody's birthday. *I* think she's got a plan for the summer holidays.'

Jack groaned. 'Blow! I've got a perfectly good plan too. Simply wizard. I'd better get mine in before Aunt Allie gets hers.'

'What's yours?' asked Dinah, with interest. Jack always had wonderful plans, though not many of them came to anything.

'Well – I thought we could all go off together on our bikes, taking a tent with us – and camp out in a different place each night,' said Jack. 'It would be super.'

The others looked at him scornfully. 'You suggested that *last* hols and the hols before,' said Dinah. 'Mother said "No" then, and she's not likely to say "Yes" now. It *is* a good plan, going off absolutely on our own like that – but ever since we've had so many adventures Mother simply won't hear of it.'

'Couldn't your mother come with us?' suggested Lucy-Ann hopefully.

'Now *you're* being silly,' said Dinah. 'Mother's a dear – but grown-ups are so frightfully particular about things. We'd have to put our macs on at the first spot of rain, and coats if the sun went in, and I wouldn't be surprised if we didn't each have to have an umbrella strapped to our bike-handles.'

The others laughed. 'I suppose it *wouldn't* do to ask Aunt Allie too, then,' said Lucy-Ann. 'What a pity!'

'What a pity, what a pity,' agreed Kiki at once. 'Wipe your feet and shut the door, where's your hanky, naughty boy!'

'Kiki's got the idea, all right!' said Philip. 'That's the kind of thing that even the nicest grown-ups say, isn't it, Kiki, old bird?'

'Bill isn't like that,' said Lucy-Ann at once. 'Bill's fine.'

Everyone agreed at once. Bill Cunningham, or Bill Smugs as he had first called himself to them, was their very firm friend, and had shared all their adventures with them. Sometimes they had dragged him into them, and sometimes it was the other way round – he had got into one and they had followed. It really did seem, sometimes, as Mrs Mannering said, that adventures cropped up wherever Bill and the children were.

'*I* had an idea for these hols too,' said Philip. 'I thought it would be pretty good fun to camp down by the river, and look for otters. I've never had an otter for a pet. Lovely things they are. I thought—'

'You *would* think of a thing like that,' said Dinah, half crossly. 'Just because you're mad on all kinds of creatures from fleas to – to . . .'

'Elephants,' said Jack obligingly.

'From fleas to elephants, you think everyone else is,' said Dinah. 'What a frightful holiday – looking for wet, slimy otters – and having them in the tent at night, I suppose – and all kinds of other horrible things too.'

'Shut up, Dinah,' said Philip. 'Otters aren't horrible. They're lovely. You should just see them swimming under the water. And by the way, I'm *not* mad on fleas. *Or* mosquitoes. *Or* horse-flies. I think they're interesting, but you can't say I've ever had things like that for pets.'

'What about those earwigs you had once – that escaped out of the silly cage you made for them? Ugh! And that stag beetle that did tricks? And that—'

'Oh, gosh! Now we're off!' said Jack, seeing one of the familiar quarrels breaking out between Philip and hot-headed Dinah. 'I suppose we're going to listen to a long list of Philip's pets now! Anyway, here comes Aunt Allie.

We can ask her what she thinks of our holiday ideas. Get yours in first, Philip.'

Mrs Mannering came in, with a booklet in her hand. She smiled round at the four children, and Kiki put up her crest in delighted welcome.

'Wipe your feet and shut the door,' she said, in a friendly tone. 'One, two, three, GO!' She made a noise like a pistol shot after the word 'go', and Mrs Mannering jumped in fright.

'It's all right, Mother – she keeps doing that ever since she came to our school sports, and heard the starter yelling to us, and letting off his pistol,' grinned Philip. 'Once she made the pistol-shot noise just when we were all in a line, ready to start – and off we went long before time! You should have heard her cackle. Bad bird!'

'Naughty Polly, poor Polly, what a pity, what a pity,' said Kiki. Jack tapped her on the beak.

'Be quiet. Parrots should be seen and not heard. Aunt Allie, we've just been talking about holiday plans. I thought it would be a super idea if you'd let us all go off on our bikes – ride where we liked and camp out each night. I know you've said we couldn't when I asked you before, but—'

'I say "No" again,' said Mrs Mannering very firmly.

'Well, Mother, could we go off to the river and camp there, because I want to find out more about the otters?' said Philip, not taking any notice of Dinah's scowl. 'You see—'

'*No*, Philip,' said his mother, just as firmly as before. 'And you know why I won't let you go on expeditions like that. I should have thought you would have given up asking me by now.'

'But *why* won't you let us go?' wailed Lucy-Ann. 'We shall be quite safe.'

'Now, Lucy-Ann, you know perfectly well that as soon as I let you four out of my sight when holidays come, you *immediately* – yes, *immediately* – fall into the most frightful adventures imaginable.' Mrs Mannering sounded quite fierce. 'And I am quite determined that these holidays you are not going off *any*where on your own, so it's just no good your asking me.'

'But, Mother, that's just silly,' said Philip in dismay. 'You speak as if we go out *looking* for adventures. We don't. And I ask you – what possible adventure could we fall into if we just went down to the river to camp? Why, you could come and see us for yourself every evening if you wanted to.'

'Yes – and the very first evening I came I should find you all spirited away somewhere, and mixed up with robbers and spies or rogues of some kind,' said his mother. 'Think of some of your holidays – first you get lost down an old copper mine on a deserted island, then another time you get shut up in the dungeons of an old castle, mixed up with spies—'

'Oooh yes – and another time we got into the wrong aeroplane and were whisked off to the Valley of

Adventure,' said Lucy-Ann, remembering. 'That was when we found all those amazing stolen statues hidden in caves – how their eyes gleamed when we saw them! I thought they were alive, but they weren't.'

'And the next time we went off with Bill to the bird-islands,' said Jack. 'That was grand. We had two tame puffins – do you remember, Philip?'

'Huffin and Puffin,' put in Kiki at once.

'Quite right, old bird,' said Philip. 'Huffin and Puffin they were. I loved them.'

'You may have gone to look for birds – but you found a whole nest of rogues,' said his mother. 'Gun-runners! Terribly dangerous.'

'Well, Mother, what about last summer hols?' said Dinah. '*You* nearly got caught up in *that* adventure!'

'Horrible!' said Mrs Mannering with a shiver. 'That awful mountain with its weird secrets – and the mad King of the Mountain – you nearly didn't escape from there. No – I tell you quite definitely that you can never again go off anywhere by yourselves. I'm always coming with you!'

There was a silence at this. All four children were very fond of Mrs Mannering – but they did like being on their own for some part of each holidays.

'Well – Aunt Allie – suppose Bill came with us – wouldn't that be all right?' asked Lucy-Ann. 'I do always feel safe with Bill.'

'Bill can't be trusted to keep out of adventures either,'

said Mrs Mannering. 'He's grand, I know, and I'd trust him more than anyone else in the world. But when you and he get together there's just no knowing what will happen. So, these holidays, I've made a very safe plan – and dear old Bill isn't in it, so perhaps we shall keep away from danger and extraordinary happenings.'

'What's your plan, Mother?' said Dinah nervously. '*Don't* say we're going to a seaside hotel or anything like that. They'd never take Kiki.'

'I'm taking you all for a cruise on a big ship,' said Mrs Mannering, and she smiled. 'I know you'll like that. It's tremendous fun. We shall call at all sorts of places, and see all kinds of strange and exciting things. And I shall have you under my eye, in one place all the time – the ship will be our home for some time, and if we get off at various ports we shall all go in a party together. There won't be a chance of any strange adventure.'

The four children looked at one another. Kiki watched them. Philip spoke first.

'It does sound rather exciting, Mother! Yes, it really does. We've never been on a really big ship before. Of course, I shall miss having any *animals* . . .'

'Oh, Philip – surely you can go without your everlasting menagerie of creatures!' cried Dinah. 'I must say it'll be a great relief to *me* to know you haven't got mice somewhere about you, or lizards, or slow-worms! Mother, it sounds super, I think. Thanks awfully for thinking up something so exciting.'

'Yes – it sounds smashing,' said Jack. 'We'll see no end of birds I've never seen before.'

'Jack's happy so long as he's somewhere that will provide him with birds,' said Lucy-Ann with a laugh. 'What with Philip with his craze for all kinds of creatures, and Jack with his passion for birds, it's a good thing we two girls haven't got crazes for anything as well. Aunt Allie, it's a wizard plan of yours. When do we go?'

'Next week,' said Mrs Mannering. 'That will give us plenty of time to get our things ready and packed. It will be very warm on the cruise, so we must get plenty of thin clothes to wear. White's the best thing – it doesn't hold the heat so much. And you must all have sun-hats the whole time, so don't begin to moan about wearing hats.'

'Isn't Bill coming?' asked Philip.

'No,' said his mother firmly. 'I feel rather mean about it, because he's just finished the job he's on, and he wants a holiday. But this time he's *not* coming with us. I want a nice peaceful holiday with no adventure at all.'

'Poor Bill,' said Lucy-Ann. 'Still – I daresay he'll be glad to have a holiday without us, for a change. I say – it's going to be fun, isn't it?'

'Fun!' said Kiki, joining in, and letting off a screech of excitement. 'Fun, fun, fun!'

2

On the Viking Star

It certainly was fun getting everything ready – buying flimsy clothes and enormous hats, masses of films for the cameras, guidebooks and maps. It was to be quite a long cruise, and the ship was to go to Portugal, Madeira, French Morocco, Spain, Italy and the Aegean Islands. What a wonderful trip!

At last everything was ready. The trunks were packed and strapped. The tickets had arrived. Passports had been got, and everyone had screamed in dismay to see how hideous they looked in their passport photographs.

Kiki screamed too, just for company. She loved screeching and screaming, but she wasn't encouraged in this, so it was a fine change to scream when everyone was doing the same.

'Shut up, Kiki,' said Jack, pushing her off his shoulder. 'Fancy screaming right in my ear like that! It's enough to make me stone deaf. Aunt Allie, will Kiki want a passport?'

'Of course not,' said Mrs Mannering. 'I'm not even sure she will be allowed to go with us.'

Jack stared at her in the greatest dismay. 'But – *I* can't go if Kiki doesn't. I couldn't leave her behind. She'd be miserable.'

'Well, I'll write and ask if you can take her,' said Mrs Mannering. 'But if the answer is no, you are *not* to make a fuss, Jack. I've gone to a lot of trouble to arrange this trip, and I can't have you upsetting it just because of Kiki. I can't imagine that she will be allowed to go – I'm sure passengers would object to a noisy bird like that.'

'She can be awfully quiet if she wants to,' said poor Jack. Kiki chose that moment to have a fit of hiccups. She hiccuped very well, and it always annoyed Mrs Mannering.

'Stop that, Kiki,' she ordered. Kiki stopped and looked reproachfully at Mrs Mannering. She began to cough, a small but hollow cough, copied from the gardener.

Mrs Mannering tried not to laugh. 'The bird is so *idiotic*,' she said. 'Quite crazy. Now, where did I put that list of things that I've got to do before we go?'

'One, two, three, GO!' shouted Kiki, and Jack just stopped her making a noise like a pistol shot. Mrs Mannering went out of the room, and Jack spoke solemnly to Kiki.

'Kiki, I may have to go without you, old bird. I can't

upset all the arrangements at the last minute because of you. But I'll do what I can, so cheer up.'

'God save the Queen,' said Kiki, feeling that it must be a solemn moment by the look on Jack's face. 'Poor Polly, naughty Polly!'

The last few days went by slowly. Lucy-Ann complained about it. 'Why is it that time always goes so slowly when you're wanting something to happen quickly? It's sickening. Thursday will never come!'

Jack was not so excited as the others, because a letter had come saying that parrots could not be taken on board. All four children were very sorry about it, and Jack looked really worried. But he did not grumble about it, or worry Mrs Mannering. She was sorry for him and offered to arrange with a woman in the village to look after Kiki for him.

'She used to have a parrot of her own,' she said. 'I expect she'd enjoy having Kiki.'

'No, thanks, Aunt Allie. I'll arrange something,' said Jack. 'Don't let's talk about it!'

So Mrs Mannering said no more, and even when Kiki sat on the tea table and picked all the currants out of the cake before anyone noticed, she did not say a word.

On Wednesday all five went off in Mrs Mannering's car to Southampton, followed by another with the baggage. They were in a great state of excitement. Everyone was in charge of something to carry, and Lucy-Ann kept

looking at her package anxiously to make sure she still
had it.

They were to stay at a hotel for the night and embark
on the ship at half past eight in the morning, to catch the
tide. They would be away at eleven o'clock, steaming
steadily towards France – what an excitement!

They all had a very good dinner at the hotel, and then
Mrs Mannering suggested going to the cinema. She felt
sure that not one of the children would go to sleep if she
sent them to bed at the usual time.

'Do you mind if I go and hunt up a school friend of
mine, Aunt Allie?' said Jack. 'He lives in Southampton,
and I'd like to spring a surprise on him and go and call.'

'All right,' said Mrs Mannering. 'But you're not to be
late back. Do you want to go and see him too, Philip?'

'Who's this chappy, Jack?' asked Philip, but Jack was
halfway out of the room. A mumble came through the
door.

'What's he say?' said Philip.

'Sounded like "Porky" to me,' said Dinah.

'Porky? Who does he mean, I wonder,' said Philip.
'Somebody mad on birds, I expect. I'll come to the
cinema. I'd like to see the picture – it's got wild animals in it.'

They went off to the cinema without seeing Jack
again. He was home when they came back, reading one
of the guidebooks Mrs Mannering had bought.

'Hello! See Porky?' said Philip. He got a frown from

Jack, and was puzzled. What was Jack up to? He changed the subject quickly, and began to talk about the picture they had seen.

'Now, to bed,' said Mrs Mannering. 'Stop talking, Philip. Off you all go – and remember, up at seven o'clock sharp in the morning.'

Everyone was awake long before seven. The girls talked together, and Philip and Jack chattered away too. Philip asked Jack about the night before.

'Why did you shut me up when I asked you if you'd seen Porky?' he said. 'And anyway – who *is* Porky?'

'He's that fellow called Hogsney,' said Jack. 'We called him Porky. He left ages ago. He was always wanting to borrow Kiki, don't you remember?'

'Oh, *yes*, Porky, of course,' said Philip. 'I'd almost forgotten him. Jack, what's up? You look sort of secretive!'

'Don't ask me any questions, because I don't want to answer them,' said Jack.

'You're being jolly mysterious,' said Philip. '*I* believe it's something to do with Kiki. You kept putting us all off when we asked you what you'd done with her. We thought you were feeling upset about it, so we didn't press you.'

'Well, don't press me now,' said Jack. 'I don't want to say anything at the moment.'

'All right,' said Philip, giving it up. 'I know you're up to something, though. Come on – let's get up. It's not seven yet, but we can't lie in bed on a morning as fine as this.'

They were all on the boat at just after half past eight. Mrs Mannering found their cabins. There were three in a row – a single one for her, and two double ones for the others.

Lucy-Ann was delighted with them. 'Why, they are just like proper little rooms,' she said. 'Jack, is your cabin like ours? Look, we've even got hot and cold water taps.'

'We've got an electric fan going in our cabin,' said Philip appearing at the door. 'It's wizard – lovely and cool. You've got one too.'

'The water is only just below our porthole,' said Dinah, looking out. 'If the sea got at all rough it would slop into the hole!'

'It would be well and truly screwed up before that happened!' said Philip. 'I'm glad we're at the waterline – it will be cooler in this warm weather. I say, isn't this super! I'm longing to sail off.'

They all went to see Mrs Mannering's cabin, which was the same as theirs but smaller. Then they went to explore the ship. She was quite big, but not tremendous, and was white from top to bottom – white funnels, white rails, white sides.

Her name was on each of the white lifeboats slung at the sides of the deck – *Viking Star*. Lucy-Ann read it a dozen times over.

'We shall have lifeboat drill tomorrow, I expect,' said Mrs Mannering, joining them on their exploration.

'There are big lifebelt jackets in our cabin cupboards,' said Lucy-Ann. 'I suppose you tie them round you.'

'You slip them over your head, so that half the jacket is at your front and half behind – and then you tie it firmly round you with the tapes,' said Mrs Mannering. 'You'll have to put it on tomorrow for lifeboat drill.'

It all sounded very exciting. They went round the ship, thrilled with everything. There was the sports deck, where someone was already playing quoits with thick rings of rope, and two others were playing deck tennis. 'Fancy being able to play games like this on board ship!' said Dinah.

'There's a cinema down below,' said Mrs Mannering, 'and a writing room, and library and lounge, and an enormous dining room!'

'And gosh, look – here's a swimming pool on the ship itself!' cried Jack in amazement as they came to a beautiful pool at one end of the ship, shimmering blue with water.

The ship's siren suddenly hooted twice very loudly. Lucy-Ann almost fell into the swimming pool with surprise. Mrs Mannering laughed.

'Oh, Lucy-Ann – did it make you jump? It made me jump too.'

'What a terrific noise!' said Lucy-Ann. 'My goodness,

it's a good thing Kiki isn't here. If she began to hoot like that siren she'd be impossible.'

'Shut up, idiot,' said Dinah in a low voice. 'Don't remind Jack we're going off without her.'

Lucy-Ann glanced round for Jack, but he wasn't there. 'Where's he gone?' she asked Dinah. But nobody had seen him go.

'He's somewhere about,' said Philip. 'I say, we must be sailing soon. Look – they're taking up the gangways. We'll soon be off!'

'Let's stand at this side and wave to all the people,' said Lucy-Ann. She leaned over the rail and watched the people crowded together on the dockside below. They were shouting and waving. Suddenly Lucy-Ann gave a squeal.

'Look! *Look!* There's somebody with a parrot *just* like Kiki! Honestly, it is. Where's Jack? I *must* tell him. Blow, he's nowhere to be seen!'

The engines of the ship had now started up, and the children felt a vibration under their feet. Lucy-Ann strained her eyes to look at the parrot that was so very like Kiki.

'It *is* Kiki!' she cried. 'Kiki! Kiki! Goodbye! I'm sure it's you!'

The parrot was chained to a young man's wrist. Whether it was making a noise or not the children could not tell because of the hullabaloo going on. It certainly was remarkably like Kiki.

'We're off! We've moved away from the quay!' cried Philip. 'Hurrah, we're off!' He waved madly to everyone. Lucy-Ann waved too, and watched the parrot. It was getting smaller as the ship moved away towards the open water. Its owner seemed to be having trouble with it. It was flapping its wings, and pecking at him.

Then it suddenly rose into the air – the chain parted – and the parrot sailed right over the stretch of water between quay and ship, screeching madly.

'It *is* Kiki, it is, it is!' yelled Lucy-Ann. 'Jack, where are you? JACK!'

3

Everyone settles in

Dinah, Lucy-Ann and Philip rushed to find Jack. The parrot had reached the ship, and they had lost sight of it. They were all certain it was Kiki, and Philip had a shrewd idea that Jack would not be quite so surprised about it as they themselves were.

Jack was nowhere to be found. It was most exasperating. They hunted for him everywhere, and at last Lucy-Ann thought of his cabin. 'He might be there,' she said. 'Though why he wants to go and shut himself up there just at the exciting moment when the ship is leaving Southampton, I really can't imagine! And where's the parrot? She seems to have disappeared too.'

They went down the stairs to the cabins and found their way to the passage where theirs were. They flung open Jack's door and crowded in. 'Jack! Are you here? What do you think we've just seen?'

They stopped in surprise at what they saw. Jack was sitting on his bed in the cabin, and Kiki was on his shoulder, making a curious crooning noise into his ear, pulling at it gently.

'Gosh!' said Philip. 'So she found you. I suppose it *is* Kiki?'

'Of course, idiot,' said Jack. 'What a bit of luck, wasn't it? Old Porky brough her down to the quay to see me off, chained to his wrist – and she broke the chain and flew over to me! Came into my porthole too – brainy old bird!'

'*Porky?* The boy you used to know at school! Did you give Kiki to *him* to mind for you?' said Lucy-Ann, amazed. 'But – how did she get down here?'

'I brought her in the car yesterday,' said Jack, putting one hand over his ear so that Kiki could not nibble it. 'She was in the picnic basket I was carrying, as quiet as a mouse. I was terrified one of you would ask me to open the basket and get you out something to eat!'

'But I say – won't Porky be upset to have her escape like that?' said Dinah.

'And *how* did she know you were here, if you were down in your cabin?' wondered Lucy-Ann. 'Perhaps she heard me call her. That must have been it – she heard me yelling "Kiki! Kiki!", broke her chain in her excitement and flew over – and by a lucky chance she chose your very porthole!'

'You'd better tell Aunt Allie all that,' said Jack, with a grin. 'It makes a very fine story – better than mine!'

The three stared at him in silence. 'You're a determined old fraud, Jack,' said Philip at last. 'You arranged it all; I bet you did! Yes, even arranged for the chain to snap and for Kiki to see or hear you at your porthole.'

Jack grinned again. 'Well, I think Lucy-Ann's idea is very good – shouting to Kiki like that and making her so excited that she flew across to the ship. Anyway, she's here, and here she stays. I'd better keep her down in the cabin, I think.'

They all made a fuss of old Kiki, who enjoyed it very much indeed. She couldn't understand the noise the vibration of the engines made, and kept cocking her head on one side to listen. She tried an imitation, but not a very good one.

'Now don't you do any funny noises,' Jack warned her. 'You don't want to be hauled up before the Captain, do you?'

'Pop goes the weasel,' said Kiki, and pecked his ear. Then she suddenly gave a most realistic sneeze.

'Don't,' said Jack. 'Use your handkerchief! Gosh, Kiki, I couldn't have gone without you.'

Everyone was pleased to know that Kiki was safely with them. They broke the news as gently as possible to Mrs Mannering. She listened in annoyance, but it did not seem to occur to her for one moment that Kiki's arrival was anything but an unfortunate accident. She sighed.

'All right. If she's here, she's here. But for goodness' sake, Jack, keep her locked up in the cabin. You really will get into trouble if the passengers complain about her, and she may be sent to the crew's deck and put in a cage if you don't keep a firm hand on her.'

So Kiki was locked into the cabin, and passed the first day wondering whether *she* was giddy, or whether there was a slight earthquake going on all the time. She had no idea she was in a big ship, and could not understand its movements, though she had many a time been in small boats.

The first day seemed lovely and long. The *Viking Star* slid easily through the calm, blue water, her engines purring sweetly, leaving behind her a creamy wake that seemed to have no end, but to stretch right back to the horizon itself. England was soon left behind. The first stop was to be Lisbon in Portugal.

It was fun to go down to meals in the big dining room and choose what they liked from the long menu. It was fun to go up on the sports deck and play deck tennis and try to keep their balance as they ran for the rubber ring. It was even fun to go to bed – because it meant snuggling down into a narrow, bunk-like bed, turning out the light, feeling the breeze from the electric fan cooling their hot bodies and hearing the plish-plish-plash of the water just below their portholes.

'Lovely!' said Lucy-Ann before she fell asleep. 'I hope this trip doesn't turn into an adventure. I like it as it is. It's quite exciting enough without having an adventure.'

It wasn't quite so nice in the Bay of Biscay! The sea

was rough and choppy there, and the boat pitched and tossed and rolled. Mrs Mannering didn't like it at all. She stayed in her cabin, but the four children were as right as rain. They turned up to every meal in the dining room, and ate steadily right down the menu. They would even have gone up to try and play deck tennis on the sports deck if one of the stewards had not firmly forbidden them to.

And then, quite suddenly as it seemed, everything changed. The sea grew blue and calm, the sun shone out very hotly indeed, the sky was brilliant, and every officer and man appeared in spotless white.

Mrs Mannering felt all right again – and Kiki grew very, very impatient at being kept in the cabin. She was already great friends with the steward and stewardess who looked after the cabins. They had soon got over their astonishment at finding her in Jack's cabin.

They had not seen her at first. She was sitting behind the little curtain that hung at the side of the porthole, which Jack had to keep shut in case Kiki flew out. It was the stewardess who heard her first. She had come in to make the beds.

Kiki watched her slyly from behind the curtain. Then she spoke in a firm and decided voice.

'Put the kettle on.'

The stewardess was startled. She looked round at the door, thinking that someone must be there speaking to her. But nobody was.

Kiki gave a loud hiccup. 'Pardon,' she said. The stewardess felt alarmed. She looked all round. She opened the cupboard door.

'What a pity, what a pity!' said Kiki, in such a mournful voice that the stewardess could bear it no longer and flew to find the steward. He was a dour and determined Scot with very little patience.

He came into the cabin and looked round. 'What's to do, wumman?' he said to the stewardess. 'What's scairt ye? There's naught here.'

Kiki gave a loud cough, and then sneezed violently. 'Pardon,' she said. 'Where's your hanky?'

Now it was the steward's turn to look amazed. He stared all round the cabin. Kiki gave a loud and realistic yawn. She had a wonderful collection of noises. She couldn't resist looking round the curtain to see how her performance was going.

The steward saw her and strode over to the porthole. 'Now look ye here – it's a parrot!' he said. 'Did ever ye hear the like? A fine and clever bird it must be to do all that! Well, Polly – you're a clever wee bird, that's what you are!'

Kiki flew to the top of the cupboard and looked at the steward and stewardess, first out of one eye and then out of the other. Then she made a noise like the dinner-gong being beaten for the ship's meals. At the end she went off into one of her cackles of laughter.

'It fair beats ye, doesn't it?' said the Scots steward,

amazed. 'A rare, bonny bird it is. The laddie that owns it should think shame on himself to keep it shut up here.'

'It scared me, right enough,' said the stewardess. 'I wonder if it would like a grape. My great-aunt's parrot loved grapes. I'll go and get some.'

Pretty soon Kiki was enjoying some black grapes, and when Jack came along to see her, he found the cabin floor scattered with grape pips, and two admiring people gaping at Kiki in delight.

'Dirty bird!' said Jack sternly, looking down at the pips. 'You come down off that cupboard and pick up these pips.'

'Pips,' said Kiki. 'Pops. Pip goes the weasel.'

'I hope she hasn't been annoying you,' said Jack to the stewardess.

'Oh, she's wonderful,' said the woman. 'I never saw such a clever bird. You ought to take her up and show her off.'

It wasn't very long before Jack did take her up to the deck above on his shoulder, much to the surprise and amusement of all the passengers. Kiki had a wonderful time showing off. The only thing she couldn't bear was the hoot of the ship's siren, which always startled her so much that she fell off Jack's shoulder in fright every time she heard it. She didn't know what it was or where it came from, and usually flew off to hide herself some-where whenever she heard it.

She came to the lifeboat drill, and Lucy-Ann was

certain she was upset because she had not a small life-jacket to wear. They all put theirs on, went to their right lifeboat and listened to a short talk from one of the officers about what they were to do if danger arose. Lucy-Ann hoped fervently that it wouldn't.

'We're going to land in Lisbon tomorrow,' said Mrs Mannering. 'But none of you is to wander off alone. I'm not going to have any adventure starting up. You'll all keep close to me – please understand *that*!'

4

Philip collects a pet

Soon the days began to slip by quickly. After Lisbon Lucy-Ann and Dinah lost count of them. They did not even know if the day was Monday, Tuesday or any other. They knew Sunday because everyone went into the big lounge then and listened to the captain taking a short church service.

For days they saw no land. Philip grew very excited when a shoal of flying fish flew out of the sea and stayed up in the air for some time. They were lovely little things.

'What makes them do that?' wondered Lucy-Ann.

'Just being chased by some hungry big fish,' said Philip. 'Wouldn't you leap out of the water and try and fly through the air if an enormous fish was after you, Lucy-Ann? Gosh, I wish one of the fish would fly on deck. I'd just love to see it close to.'

'Well, you couldn't possibly make it a pet, thank goodness, because it would die in your pocket,' said

Dinah. 'It seems unusual for you to be without any pets at all, Philip. Very nice!'

But she spoke too soon, because Philip collected a pet two days later! They had called at Madeira, left that island, and gone on to French Morocco. It was there that Philip collected his strange little pet.

The children liked French Morocco. They especially liked the bazaars, although the air was so strongly scented that Mrs Mannering said it made her feel faint, and she walked along with smelling salts pressed to her nose. The children soon got used to the air, though Kiki didn't, judging by the number of 'Poohs' she said. 'Pooh! Gah! Pooh!'

Dinah tried out her French on the black-eyed traders, and was pleased when they understood. She bought a tiny brooch, and Lucy-Ann bought a blue vase.

'Don't you see anything *you* like?' she asked Philip. He shook his head.

'I don't want things like that. Now if I could see something really exciting – say an old dagger – or, I tell you what! Something I've always wanted and never had.'

'What's that?' asked Lucy-Ann, determined to buy it for him if only she could see it.

'You'll laugh – but I've always wanted a ship in a bottle,' said Philip.

'I've never even seen one,' said Lucy-Ann, astonished. 'A ship *inside* a bottle, do you mean? What a peculiar thing? How is it put there?'

'I don't know,' said Philip. 'It's daft of me to want it, really – it's just one of those ideas you get, you know.'

'I'll be sure to look out for one for you wherever we go,' promised Lucy-Ann. 'Oh, do look at Kiki. She's taking sweets from those little children there. She'll make herself sick again!'

Mrs Mannering insisted that they should all stay close to her, and keep with the ship's party. The four children wished they could explore by themselves, for they liked the people and their strange, dark, narrow little shops.

'Certainly not,' said Mrs Mannering. 'Why, didn't you hear what happened to the man at the next table to ours on the ship? He and his wife went off by themselves in a taxi to visit some place or other – and the driver took them to a deserted hill, and wouldn't take them back to the ship till they had given him all the money they had!'

'Gracious,' said Lucy-Ann, surprised.

'He brought them back just as the gangway was being drawn up,' went on Mrs Mannering, 'so they had no time to make any complaint. *Now* you know why I want you to keep with the ship's party. No more adventures for you, if I can help it! It would be just like you all to disappear somewhere, get into awful danger and put a few more grey hairs into my head!'

'You haven't *really* got very many,' said Lucy-Ann. 'Just about one for each of our adventures, that's all! I *will* keep near to you, Aunt Allie. I don't want an adventure either.'

The next day there was to be a trip by motor coach to a famous place inland – an old town on the edge of the desert. 'The motor coaches will be here on the quay at half past ten,' Mrs Mannering told the four. 'Be sure to wear your sun-hats. It will be terribly hot.'

It was on that trip that Philip collected his new pet. The motor coaches duly arrived and everyone crowded into them, feeling extremely hot. Off they went at top speed down a sandy road that for a time seemed to run through what looked like a bare desert. Large cactus plants grew by the roadside. Lucy-Ann thought they looked ugly and spiteful with their numerous prickles and fat bulging bodies.

After two hours they came to the old town. Its ancient arches and towers seemed to spring up suddenly out of the sand. Little dark-eyed children, with hardly anything on, ran to meet them, their hands held out.

'Penn-ee, penn-ee,' they said, and Kiki echoed them at once. 'Penn-ee, penn-ee!'

They all went into the narrow street of the old town. The guide took them to an ancient building and began to drone on about its history. Then one by one the party climbed steep, winding steps up an enormous tower.

Halfway up Philip looked out of a great stone window. It had no glass, of course. The wall was so thick that he could sit on the window sill with his legs stretched right out. He hung on to the side of the window and slid forward to look down.

Far below he could see a little crowd of excited children. They were pointing upwards and chattering. Some of them were throwing stones.

'Now what are those little scamps throwing stones at?' thought Philip. 'If it's something alive I'll knock their heads together!'

He slid down from the enormous window sill and ran down the great winding stairs. A stone flew through a window opening not far from the bottom, and he stopped.

He heard a small whimpering noise and, hidden in a corner of the window opening, he saw a little heap of brown fur. He went over to it. What could it be?

Click! A stone flew near him. Blow those kids! He stepped to the window and looked down sternly. 'You stop that!' he shouted. 'Do you hear me? Stop it!'

The small children looked in consternation at this sudden apparition. They disappeared in a hurry. Philip reached over to the brown bundle. A small wizened face peeped out at him with mournful brown eyes. Then it was covered by tiny hands.

'Why – it's a monkey – a tiny monkey!' thought Philip. He knew how scared the small creatures were, and he was afraid of frightening this poor little mistreated animal. He had seen plenty of monkeys in that part of the country already, but not near – they always kept well out of the way.

Philip spoke to the small creature in what Lucy-Ann

called his 'special animal voice.' It uncovered its funny little face again, and then, with one bound, was cuddling into the boy's shoulder, nestling against his neck, trembling. He put up a cautious hand and rubbed its soft fur.

No animal had ever been able to resist Philip's magic. Horses, dogs, cats, snakes, insects, birds – they came to him at once trustingly and confidingly. Not one could resist him. It was a gift that everyone marvelled at and envied him for.

Philip sat down on the broad window sill and talked to the scared and miserable little monkey. It chattered back in a high, cheeping little voice. It looked at him shyly out of childlike brown eyes. Its tiny brown fingers wound themselves round one of his. It was Philip's devoted slave from that moment.

When the others came pattering down the stairs in front of the rest of the party, they were astonished to see the small monkey cuddling up to Philip.

'There – I knew he'd get hold of something sooner or later!' said Dinah. 'Ugh! A nasty, dirty, smelly little monkey, full of fleas too, I expect.'

'Well, it *is* dirty and smelly, and I'm sure it's got fleas,' said Philip. 'But it isn't nasty. It's been stoned by those wretched children down below. Both its legs are hurt.'

'Poor little thing,' said Lucy-Ann, almost in tears. Jack stroked the tiny thing's head, but that only made it shrink closer to Philip.

'You're not to take it back to the ship with you,' began

Dinah. 'I shall tell Mother if you do. I won't have a monkey in our party.'

'He's coming with me,' said Philip sternly.

Dinah began to lose her temper. 'Then I shall tell Mother I won't have it. I shall—'

'Dinah, it's so *small*, and it's *hurt*,' said Lucy-Ann, in a shaky voice. 'Don't talk like that. It's so unkind.'

Dinah flushed, and turned away. She was cross, and horrified at the thought of having a monkey 'tagging along' with them, as she put it – but she did not want to go against the other three. She said no more, though she was unhappy for the rest of the day.

How Philip hid the monkey till he got back to the ship only he knew. The fact is that no one even noticed it. Jack and Lucy-Ann helped him valiantly by standing in front of him whenever they thought anyone might see the monkey. Dinah would not help, but on the other hand she did nothing to give the secret away.

Back in the cabin, the three children pored over the tiny creature. 'It's not even a grown monkey,' said Philip. 'How those children could stone a little thing like this beats me. But I suppose in every country there are cruel and unkind people – after all, we've seen boys back at home throwing stones at a cat. Look – its legs are bruised and cut, but they're not broken. I can soon get those right. I wonder if it would let me wash it – it's so dirty.'

The little thing would let Philip do anything in the world he wanted to. The children spent two hours washing and drying it gently. Jack brought a small shoe-brush to brush its fluffy fur. It let Philip put iodine on its cuts and gave only a tiny whimper.

'There!' said the boy. 'You look fine. What's your name?'

The monkey chattered something, and the children listened. 'It sounds as if he's saying "Micky-micky-mick",' said Lucy-Ann.

'Right. If he thinks his name is Micky, Micky it is,' said Philip. 'I wonder what Kiki will think of him.'

'She won't like him much,' said Jack. 'She'll be jealous. Good thing we left her in the girls' cabin. She'd screech the place down if she saw us washing and brushing Micky.'

Kiki certainly was most amazed to see Micky on Philip's shoulder that night. She stared, and then, just as Jack had said, she screeched – one of her very best express-train screeches. Mrs Mannering put her head in at the cabin door to protest.

She suddenly caught sight of the monkey and stepped forward in surprise, wondering if she had seen aright. 'Oh, Philip! You oughtn't to have brought it back to the ship. What a tiny thing!'

'Mother, some children were stoning it. I had to bring it away,' said Philip. His mother looked at him. It was just exactly the kind of thing Philip's father had done when he was alive. How could she scold him for something that was in his very blood?

'Well – I don't know if a fuss will be made if you keep him on the ship,' she said, stroking the monkey's head. 'What does Dinah say about it?'

'She was very cross at first, but she didn't say much,' said Lucy-Ann. 'She's still in our cabin, I think. She'll get over Micky. She'll have to.'

'Micky – Kiki – Micky – Kiki – Micky – Kiki,' said Kiki triumphantly, as if she had suddenly discovered something very clever. She loved words that sounded the same. 'Micky – Kiki, Micky – Kiki—'

'Shut up, Kiki,' said Philip. 'I say, what a pity he's called Micky – we'll never stop Kiki saying those two words now. But he *is* Micky. We can't alter his name now.'

So Micky he was, and in a day or two he was everyone's friend – yes, even Dinah's! He had such a dear, comical face that it was impossible not to like him when he looked at you out of mournful brown eyes.

'He's such a baby and yet he's got such a wise, wizened little face,' said Lucy-Ann. 'And I do like his tiny fingers – just like ours! Don't you, Dinah?'

'Well – he's not as awful as I thought he was at first,' admitted Dinah. 'I can't say I want him sitting on my shoulder all day long, like Philip – and I'm sure he's still got fleas – but he's really not bad.'

'He *hasn't* got fleas,' said Philip, annoyed. 'Don't keep saying that.'

Micky soon recovered his spirits, and from being a

gentle, confiding little thing, he became a mischievous, chattering madcap. He leapt about the cabin as lightly as a squirrel, and Dinah was always scared he would take a flying jump on to her shoulder. But he didn't. He was wise enough not to do that!

Kiki was alarmed to see these acrobatics, and when the two were together in the same cabin she always turned to face Micky, so that she could jab him with her beak if he leapt at her. But he left her alone, and took very little notice. She didn't like that at all!

She took to calling his name in Philip's voice, which she could imitate perfectly. 'Micky! Micky!'

The monkey would look round at once, but would see no Philip. 'Micky!' Kiki would say again, and the monkey would begin to leap all over the place, trying to find Philip.

Then Kiki would cackle with laughter, and Micky would go off in disgust and sit on the porthole sill with his back to Kiki, looking through the thick glass out to sea.

Kiki certainly had the best of it because she soon found that she could make noises that terrified Micky. If she barked like a dog the little creature went nearly frantic with fright. He was puzzled too. He watched Kiki closely, and soon realised that no dog barked unless Kiki was in the cabin. Then was Kiki some kind of bird-dog?

The next time she barked she followed it with a fierce

growl. This was too much for Micky. He picked up a tablet of soap from the basin and flung it at the surprised Kiki. It hit her full on the beak and she gave a squawk of alarm and nearly fell off her perch.

Micky sent a toothbrush after the soap, and then the tooth-mug. He was a very fine shot, and soon Kiki was flying round the cabin trying to find a place to shelter from the volley of articles that Micky was sending after her – hairbrushes, combs, a roll of film, anything he could get hold of!

Philip stopped the battle when he came in. 'Micky! Pick them all up!' he said sternly. 'What did Kiki do to you to make you lose your temper like that? Bad Micky!'

'Naughty Micky, bad boy!' said Kiki at once, and went off into one of her cackles of laughter. Micky picked everything up humbly. Then he went to sit on Philip's shoulder as usual. Kiki was jealous. She flew to his other shoulder.

The monkey chattered at her. Kiki chattered back, in exactly the same monkey voice as Micky used. He stared in amazement, and answered excitedly. Philip listened, amused.

'Well, I don't really know if you understand one another or not,' he said. 'But it's just as well you should. I don't want to find my cabin strewn with all my belongings each time I come into it. So just be friends! Do you hear, Kiki and Micky?'

'Pooh,' said Kiki, in a friendly voice, and nibbled at him.

'Pooh to you!' said Philip. 'And kindly stop nibbling my ear!'

5

Lucian arrives

The children soon felt that the *Viking Star* was their home – a floating home, containing everything they wanted except the open countryside. They got to know every nook and cranny on the ship, they explored the engine room under the eye of Mac, the chief engineer, and they were even allowed up on the bridge by the first officer, a very great honour.

Mrs Mannering made friends on the ship with two or three people she liked. There were only a few children on board besides Jack and the others, and they were much younger and so spoilt that nobody wanted to have much to do with them.

'I rather wish there were more children of your own age,' Mrs Mannering said to her four. 'It might be more fun for you.'

'Well – *we* don't want anyone else, thanks,' said Philip. 'We're all right on our own. It's bad enough having those other spoilt kids around – always wanting to mess about with Micky, and trying to get Kiki to talk to them.'

'She's too sensible,' said Jack. 'Kiki just looks at them and says "Shut up!" whenever she sees them.'

'How rude of her!' said Mrs Mannering. 'I do hope you stop her when she talks like that to the other children.'

'Well, actually I don't,' said Jack. 'She only says what I jolly well would like to say myself. Spoilt little brats! I'm going to push that nasty little yellow-haired girl into the swimming pool one of these days – coming whining round me asking me if she can hold Kiki. *Hold* Kiki! What does she think Kiki is – one of her frightful dolls?'

'You mustn't push the child into the pool,' said Mrs Mannering, horrified. 'I do agree she wants slapping – but she's only a little girl, Jack.'

'She's a human mosquito,' said Jack. 'I just wish I had a fly-swatter when she comes near.'

'Well, all the kids are getting off at the next stop,' said Philip, fondling Micky who, as usual, was on his shoulder. The boys looked a curious pair, one with a parrot on his shoulder, the other with a monkey. The passengers smiled whenever they saw them.

'I'm glad to hear those tiresome children will soon be gone,' said Dinah, who was not very fond of youngsters. 'But I expect some equally dreadful ones will embark in their place.'

She was wrong, as it happened. Only one boy embarked; no girls at all. All the spoilt youngsters left, stumbling down the gangway at Naples, screaming and complaining to the last, certainly a most unpleasant collection of small children. Jack and the others watched them go with pleasure, and Kiki screeched after them. 'Goodbye, good riddance, goodbye, good riddance!'

'Jack! She's never said that before,' said Mrs Mannering reproachfully. 'You must just have taught her!'

'Kiki only reads my thoughts, Aunt Allie,' laughed Jack. 'I say – look here – here comes Brer Rabbit!'

The children giggled as they watched a tall, gangling boy come up the gangway. His mouth certainly was exactly like a rabbit's. The front teeth stuck out, and his chin sloped backwards. He was about as old as Jack and Philip. He wore large, round glasses that magnified his eyes and made them look rather staring. He had a very amiable grin on his face as he came up the gangway.

He seemed very excited, and was talking in a mixture of English and some foreign language to a rather languid-looking lady behind him and a short, burly man who wore dark sunglasses that completely hid his eyes.

'Uncle, Aunt, we're off at last! Oh, I say, what a magnificent ship! I'm sure I shan't be seasick in her.' Then he went off into what sounded like a string of gibberish but was really a foreign language. Kiki cocked her head when she heard this string of what sounded to her like complete nonsense.

As the boy passed she spoke to him in a conversational tone, pouring out the same kind of gibberish that she had heard. The boy looked at her in amazement.

'Oh, I say! A talking parrot. Oh, I *say!*'

'Oh, I say!' repeated Kiki immediately. 'Oh, I *say!* Oh, I SAY!'

'Shut up, Kiki. Don't be rude,' said Jack.

Micky leaned forward on Philip's shoulder and sent out a stream of excited chattering to Kiki. The boy stared in delight.

'Oh, I say! A talking monkey too! What's he saying?'

'He says he thinks he's seen you somewhere before, but he can't remember where, and he wants to know if Kiki the parrot remembers,' said Philip solemnly. Lucy-Ann gave a delighted giggle. The boy stared open-mouthed, then he laughed, showing all his big teeth.

'Oh, you're pulling my leg, aren't you? But I say – what fun – a parrot that talks, and a tame monkey! Aren't you lucky!'

'Get on, Lucian, get on,' said the burly man behind him, and gave the boy a push. Lucian went forward at a run, turning round to give the four children an apologetic grin for leaving them so abruptly. The man said something in an annoyed voice to the woman with him, but as he said it in a foreign language the children didn't understand a word. They guessed at once, however, that Lucian was not very popular with his uncle!

'Well – if Rabbit is the only boy to come on board here, I suppose he'll pin himself on to us all day long,' said Philip. 'What a weed!'

'Oh, I say!' said Kiki. Jack groaned.

'Now we shall have Kiki saying that day and night. It's a good thing Micky can't talk properly – we'd never get a word in edgeways!'

The ship sailed off again into waters bluer than ever. It was pleasant to go to the bow of the ship and feel the breeze. Both Kiki and Micky liked this too.

Just as Jack and Philip had feared, the new boy tagged himself on to them whenever he could. The children always knew when he was coming because Kiki invariably gave them warning.

'Oh, I say!' she would squawk, and the four would sigh. Lucian again! He would come up grinning amiably, and settle himself beside them.

He told them all about himself immediately. He had no father or mother. His father had been English, but his mother was Greek, so he had plenty of Greek relations. He went to school in England, but spent most of his holidays with his relations. He was fourteen, nearly fifteen, he didn't like games, he loved history, and he wished his name wasn't Lucian.

'Why?' asked Dinah.

'Well – because the boys at my school change it to

Lucy-Ann,' explained Lucian. 'I mean – fancy having a name that's as girlish as that.'

'It's *my* name,' said Lucy-Ann. 'I like it.'

'Well – it's very nice for *you*,' said Lucian. 'But awful for me. Especially when they shorten it and call me Lucy.'

'Juicy Lucy!' said Kiki at once in delight. 'Juicy Lucy! Oh, I say!'

Everybody roared, even Lucian. Kiki cackled too.

'Juicy Lucy, goosey-Lucy, oh, I say!' carolled Kiki.

'Oh, I say, really – that bird of yours is a regular comic, isn't she?' said Lucian in admiration. 'Gosh, I wish I could borrow her to take back to school. I say, do *you* take her to school with you?'

'I used to,' said Jack regretfully. 'But she kept telling our form-master to wipe his feet and shut the door, and when she yelled out "Don't sniff, use your hanky" to the Head, well, that was about the end.'

'Do you remember how you put her in a cupboard once, to hide her in class – and she went off like fireworks, fizzling and popping and exploding?' said Philip with a grin. 'It was just after Guy Fawkes Day – she remembered the noises.'

Lucian listened in the greatest admiration, his wide mouth open as if he listened with that as well as with his ears.

'Oh, I say! What happened?'

'Well – we exploded too!' said Philip. 'And after that,

the master did – in a different way, of course. We had to put Kiki out to live with someone in the village. We go to see her every day, naturally, and have her on half-holidays and weekends.'

'And she always goes to every school match and cheers like anything – doesn't she, Jack?' said Lucy-Ann.

'She's a wonder,' said Lucian. 'Let me have her for a minute.'

'Look out – she won't go to strangers,' warned Jack. But Lucian was already trying to get hold of the wonderful parrot. He soon let her go. She gave him a vicious nip with her curved beak, and he yelled. To Lucy-Ann's amazement she saw tears in his eyes!

He turned and went off without a word, sucking his bleeding thumb. The others looked at one another.

'He was crying,' said Lucy-Ann, in sheer amazement that a boy of fourteen should do such a thing.

'He's a nitwit,' said Jack, trying to calm down Kiki, who had put up her crest tremendously, and was dancing angrily from one foot to another.

'Nit-wit,' said Kiki, pouncing on the word at once, 'Nit-wit, wit-nit, tit-bit, bit-nit, oh, I say!'

'You're a bad bird, nipping people like that,' scolded Jack. 'That was a nasty nip.'

'Nip-wit,' announced Kiki.

'Yes, that's about what you are – a nip-wit!' said Jack with a chuckle. 'Now don't you start, Micky! We've had enough rudery from Kiki.'

Micky had started off on one of his long strings of excited gibberish. It was comical to see how seriously and solemnly Kiki listened to this, with her head on one side.

She answered the little monkey gravely when he had finished his excited announcement, whatever it was.

'Rikky-likky-acky, icky, pop-pop-pop!' she said. The children roared. 'She thinks she's talking his language. Good old Kiki! You can't get the better of *her*,' said Philip. 'I'm glad she's more friendly with Micky now. He's such a dear.'

'He's getting awfully mischievous, though,' said Dinah, who now thought of the monkey much more kindly. 'He went into a dozen cabins yesterday, and collected all the soaps out of the basins and put them in one of the armchairs in the lounge.'

'Gracious!' said Jack. 'He'll be getting into trouble soon.'

'You mean *we* shall,' said Philip. 'I wish we could teach Kiki to keep an eye on Micky for us – but she encourages him. I'm sure it was Kiki who told the monkey to climb up the mast to the man in the crow's-nest there and give him an awful fright.'

'Micky's a dear,' said Lucy-Ann, and she tickled him under his furry chin. He looked at her with wise, sad eyes. Lucy-Ann knew he was very happy now, but she was always worried because he looked at her sorrowfully.

She only half believed Philip when he told her that all monkeys looked sad.

'There's the gong for lunch,' said Dinah thankfully. 'I feel as if it's about an hour late today, I'm so hungry. Come on, everybody!'

6

The tale of Andra's treasure

The *Viking Star* was now going off to cruise among the islands of the Aegean Sea. The water was a beautiful dark blue, and the children thought it was the nicest part of the trip, seeing the islands loom up out of the purple-blue sea.

Lucian proved himself quite useful here, because he knew that part of the sea very well. He was able to tell them about the different islands, and he was full of exciting stories of old pirates and robberies at sea, and the taking of treasure.

'See that island we're coming to,' he said. 'That's Oupos. It's only small, but it's got an old castle on it with one of the biggest dungeons in the world. The old sailors used to take prisoners at sea, and sail to Oupos, and dump their prisoners in the dungeons. Sometimes they left them there for years – till they were old men.'

'How horrible!' said Lucy-Ann. 'Have you been on Oupos?'

'Yes, once,' said Lucian. 'I saw the holes for the dungeons too. Nearly fell down one myself.'

'What do you mean – holes for the dungeons?' asked Philip.

'Well – the yard of the old castle was pitted with holes – deep, very deep holes,' explained Lucian. 'And when a prisoner was landed on the island he was dragged to the great yard and popped down the nearest hole. He fell down, down into the dungeons below, and joined the other prisoners there.'

'How awful! Couldn't he get out again?' asked Jack in horror.

'No. The only way out was up the steep, deep holes,' said Lucian. 'No one could climb up those.'

'But how were the prisoners fed?' asked Philip.

'Easy,' said Lucian. 'The guards just went to the holes each day and tipped food down.'

'I don't know whether to believe that or not,' said Jack.

'I tell you I've been on the island and seen the holes,' insisted Lucian. 'Of course, the dungeons aren't used *now* – the yard is all overgrown, and you can hardly see the dungeon holes. That's how I nearly fell down one.'

'Would you have been there till you were old?' asked Lucy-Ann.

'Of course not. My uncle would have got a rope and hauled me up,' said Lucian. 'I should probably have broken my leg, though.'

'Tell us some more tales about these old islands,' said Jack. 'I wouldn't mind visiting one or two!'

'Well, I dare say we could, if I asked my uncle,' said Lucian surprisingly.

'What do you mean? What's your uncle got to do with it?' demanded Philip. 'You talk as if he owned the islands.'

'He does own quite a few,' said Lucian. 'Didn't I tell you? It's a craze of his, I think. He buys this one and that one, explores it thoroughly – and then maybe he gets tired of it and sells it again.'

The four children looked at Lucian to see if he was telling the truth. It seemed extraordinary to them that anyone should buy and sell islands as if they were cakes or something.

'But – what does he do it for?' asked Jack. 'I mean – is he interested in old things – is he looking for antiques or something?'

'He's very interested in history,' said Lucian. 'Yes, and in old things generally. You should see his house in Athens. He's got the most marvellous collection of things from these old islands. He's crazy about them.'

The children thought about Lucian's uncle. They could not tell if he was crazy or not. He seemed an ordinary, rather cross grown-up to them, hard to size up because he always wore dark glasses and they could not see his eyes.

'You don't know what people are *thinking* if you can't see their eyes,' Lucy-Ann said, and it was true.

'I expect I get my liking for history from my uncle,' said Lucian. 'I'm always top in that. Bottom in everything else, of course. And I *loathe* games.'

'Yes, you've told us that before,' said Jack.

'But only about fifteen times,' put in Dinah.

'Oh, I say!' said Lucian. 'Sorry! It's just that I do detest them so much.'

'Sixteen times,' said Lucy-Ann.

'Goosey-Lucy,' remarked Kiki – very aptly, the children thought. They grinned at one another, Lucian *was* a goose – a silly, credulous, aggravating, tiresome goose, a nitwit and a rabbit – but he was quite harmless and sometimes really amusing.

'To come back to your uncle,' said Jack. 'Do you honestly mean he owns some of these exciting islands?'

'Oh, yes. He doesn't own Oupos now. But he owns the one we'll soon be passing. That'll be Helios. He's about finished with it now, though. He sent his men there to dig and explore, but they didn't find much.'

'What *did* they find?' asked Lucy-Ann with interest.

'Let me see – they found three magnificent vases, but that was about all,' said Lucian. 'They were cracked, of course – they nearly always are, it seems to me. He found a pair of daggers too – frightfully old I think those were. And he got a lot of rubbish too – you know, bits of broken crockery, pieces of jewellery not worth anything

– oh, yes, and he got a little carving of a goose. He gave it to me.'

'Goosey-Lucy,' put in Kiki again. She appeared to be listening hard to all Lucian's rigmarole.

'Shut up, Kiki. Don't interrupt,' said Jack. 'Go on, Lucy – I mean Lucian.'

'Oh, I say! Don't you start calling me that, Jack,' said Lucian, looking hurt.

'Don't be an ass. Get on with your story,' said Jack. He had no patience with Lucian when he began getting hurt, which happened quite a lot.

'Do you know any more stories about the islands?' asked Lucy-Ann, seeing that Lucian still looked upset.

'Well – there's the story of the Andra treasure ships,' said Lucian. 'That's supposed to be absolutely true. I've heard my uncle tell it many a time.'

'Go on – tell us,' said Philip, scratching Micky's back for him as he lay cuddled in the boy's arms, fast asleep.

'Well, it happened hundreds of years ago,' began Lucian. 'I can't remember the exact date. There was a king called Panlostes who had a kingdom on one of these islands, a large one. I expect you know that most of them had rulers of their own. Well, Panlostes had a son.'

'What was he called?' asked Lucy-Ann.

'I don't know,' said Lucian. 'Anyway this son had an accident when he was small, and he lost one eye and hurt his foot so that he limped. He wanted to marry the daughter of a king on the mainland of Greece, a girl called Andra.'

'But she wouldn't have him because he was one-eyed and limped, I suppose,' said Jack. 'And there was someone else she liked and wanted to marry.'

'Well – if you know the story . . .' began Lucian, half annoyed.

'I don't. But I know lots like it!' said Jack. 'Go on.'

'Andra's father said the girl should marry the one-eyed prince if King Panlostes would send him gold and arms and treasure worth half his kingdom,' went on Lucian, warming up again. 'So the King got ready a fleet of ships and stuffed them with riches of all kinds, and one morning they set sail from the island to go to the mainland.'

Lucy-Ann gazed out over the dark-blue sea, imagining the fleet of small ships, their sails filled with the wind, their holds packed with rich treasure. She heard the sharp commands, the creaking of the old wooden ships, the billowing, flapping noise of the sails. Lucian took another breath and continued.

'Well – the girl Andra sent word to the man she really wanted to marry to tell him about the ships. And he got ready some ships himself and set out to intercept the treasure fleet.'

'Did he find them?' asked Lucy-Ann.

'Yes, he did. But when he attacked them and finally defeated the fleet – he found no treasure!'

'Gracious! Where had it gone?' asked Dinah. 'Had they dumped it into the sea, or something?'

'No. The captain of the fleet had never meant to deliver the treasure safely. He had made up his mind to take it to an island he knew of, land it there, hide it safely and come back for it when he could. He meant to tell both Kings that he had been attacked and robbed on the way to the mainland.'

'And he *was* attacked – but he had hidden the treasure!' said Jack. 'What happened next?'

'The captain was killed and so were half the men. The rest of them made off in their ships and scattered far and wide. A search was made for the hidden treasure, but it couldn't be found.'

'Golly – was nothing more ever heard of it?' said Philip.

'Oh, yes. Some of the men thought they remembered where the island was where they had landed the treasure one night. They made up an expedition secretly and went to look for it. They quarrelled and fought – and in the end only two or three men were left. One of them had made a rough map.'

'A map of the island? Was it ever found?' asked Dinah in excitement.

'Yes. Years later. A Greek merchantman got hold of it somehow and pored over the old map till he had made some sense out of it. He made up his mind that it could refer to only five out of all the islands in the Aegean Sea – and there are heaps and heaps, you know. So he began to explore them one by one.'

'Did he find the right one?' asked Lucy-Ann, her eyes shining. 'This is a lovely story, *I* think.'

'Yes – the old story says he did find the island – and found out where the treasure was too. But before he could do anything about it, he died.'

There was a disappointed silence. 'But who got the treasure then?' asked Jack.

'Nobody,' said Lucian. 'The old merchantman never told a soul. But it's said that *some*where there's a copy of the map and plan he made. Goodness knows where! He hid it before he died, or so people say. He lived about a hundred years ago.'

'What a thrilling story!' said Dinah. 'I wish *we* could find the map. Where did the old man live? Surely the map would be hidden in the house he had?'

'I should think it's been searched from top to bottom,' said Lucian. 'I know the island he lived on. We shall come to it in a day's time. It's called Amulis.'

'Oh! Are we going to land on it?' cried Lucy-Ann. 'I'd like to!'

'Yes. We usually do call there,' said Lucian. 'It's quite a big island, with towns and villages, and some good shops that sell antiques and things. Visitors often go in parties from the ships and buy things.'

'We'll go together!' said Dinah. 'I want to buy some things – I haven't nearly enough. Come with us, Lucian, you'll really be a very great help!'

7

Lucian is very helpful

Mrs Mannering was pleased to hear that the ship was to call at the romantic island of Amulis. She, like the children, had been fascinated by all the misty-purple islands that kept looming up in the dark-blue sea. She had been dipping into Greek history, and somehow it seemed as if the Aegean Sea belonged to the past, not to the present.

The children borrowed her books and read them too. How old these islands were, and what stories they held! Lucy-Ann was fascinated by them. She stood at the deck rail and watched all day long.

'Why are there so many?' she said. 'What do you call a collection of so many islands? It's a long name, I know.'

'Archipelago,' said Mrs Mannering. 'You know, Lucy-Ann, it's said that once all these islands were joined together, making a great mainland. Then something happened, and the sea rushed into what is now the Mediterranean basin, filled it up, and drowned a lot of this mainland. Only the highest parts, the hills and mountains, were left – and they show above the water as islands – the Aegean islands we are cruising among!'

'My goodness,' said Lucy-Ann, her quick imagination showing her a great sweep of water rushing relentlessly over a land where towns and villages stood – swallowing them up one by one, drowning them – and at last leaving only the highest parts showing above the surface of the waters. 'Oh, Aunt Allie – do you mean that far below us, on the ocean bed, are the ruined remains of cities and villages? Did it happen long ago?'

'Thousands and thousands of years ago,' said Mrs Mannering. 'There wouldn't be a trace of them left now. But it explains the myriads of little islands in this sea. I'm glad we are to visit one of them.'

'You're not afraid of us falling into some exciting adventure now, are you?' said Lucy-Ann slyly. 'You think it will be safe to visit this romantic little island?'

'Quite safe,' said Mrs Mannering, laughing. 'For one thing I shall be with you.'

'We've asked Lucian to come too,' said Dinah. 'I know he's a nitwit – but he really does know about these islands, Mother. He's told us all sorts of stories about them. His uncle owns some of them.'

'Yes, I heard that he did,' said Mrs Mannering. 'I've talked to his wife – quite a nice woman. I can't say I'd like a husband who did nothing but buy up islands and dig frantically for months, then sell them and start somewhere else. He's got a bee in his bonnet, I think. Still, he certainly seems to have made some interesting finds – finds that have made him a wealthy man!'

The *Viking Star* sailed into a small port the next day. The children were hanging over the deck rail and were surprised when their ship came to a stop and anchored where she was without steaming to the jetty.

'We can't get any closer in – the jetty isn't suitable for us. We're too big,' explained one of the officers to the children. 'You'll go ashore in a motor launch.'

Sure enough a launch came out to the ship, and a score or so of passengers climbed down the ladder to the deck of the launch. The four children went, of course, and Lucian, also Mrs Mannering and some of the other interested passengers. Lucian's people did not go. They knew so much about the island that they had no desire to visit Amulis.

But to the children it was all very thrilling indeed. The motor launch sped off to the jetty where they all landed. Lucian was quite at home on the island, which he had visited before with his uncle.

'You keep with me. I can show you all the interesting things,' he said. 'And I can talk to the people too, and bargain for you if you want to buy anything.'

Lucian was certainly very, very useful. He pushed off the flock of little children who came crowding round begging for money, and sent out such a fierce stream of odd-sounding words that even Kiki was most impressed.

He knew his way about and was quite good at explaining things.

'Here's the market. The people from the hills up there bring their goods down here – look at them on the stalls – then they spend the money they get at the shops in the town. Or they go to the cinema.'

The people were a picturesque lot. They wore big hats because of the sun, and a collection of nondescript white garments that might have been anything, but which suited them quite well. The children were beautiful, Lucy-Ann thought, with their dark eyes, beautifully shaped faces and thick curling hair.

Lucian took them to an old ruined castle, but the boys were disappointed because there were no dungeons to be seen. The girls were amazed to see people apparently living in parts of the castle, together with their goats and hens.

'They're very poor islanders,' explained Lucian. 'They've got nowhere else to live. Further inland, if I'd time to take you, you'd see people living in caves in the mountainsides. They used to do that thousands of years ago too. It's strange to think those caves have sheltered people century after century.'

'Do those cave-people go to the cinema in the town?' asked Dinah.

'Oh, yes. They love it, though they can't read anything in English on the screen. The speech is translated, of course,' said Lucian. 'They live in two worlds, really –

the world of long ago, when people used caves as shelter and scraped along with their goats and hens and geese, and in the world of today, where there are motorcars and cinemas and so on.'

'A weird mixture,' said Jack. 'I shouldn't know where I was!'

'Oh, they know, all right,' said Lucian, and he paused to shout angrily at a small child who was trying slyly to pull at a ribbon Lucy-Ann was wearing in her dress. Kiki also began to scream excitedly, and Micky jumped up and down on Philip's shoulder, chattering. The child fled in terror. Lucy-Ann felt quite sorry for it.

Lucian took them to the shops. Some of them were small, secret shops, dark and full of strange goods. One shop, which was full of antiques to attract visitors, was quite big.

'You can go in here if you want to look round and buy something,' said Lucian. 'Oh, I say! Where's Micky gone?'

'Just to have a little exercise on the canopy over the shop,' said Philip. Micky was amusing, the way he often leapt off Philip's shoulder and hung on to all kinds of things nearby, scampering here and there, flinging himself through the air to some fresh place, never once falling or missing his hold. He was now galloping over the sun canopy, running from side to side, occasionally stopping to fling himself up to a window ledge overhead and then drop back. But when he saw that Philip was going into the shop below he threw himself down from the canopy and with a flying leap was back on the boy's shoulder.

'Can't get rid of you, can I?' said Philip. 'You're a bad penny, always turning up – and you do make my neck so hot!'

The shop was fascinating to the four children. They had no idea which things were genuinely old and which were not. Lucian, with the knowledge he had picked up from his uncle, pointed out a few really old things, but they were far too expensive to buy. Lucy-Ann looked at her money and asked Lucian if there was anything at all she could afford to buy.

He counted it up. It was Greek money, and Lucy-Ann had no idea of its value.

'Yes, you might buy one or two things,' he said. 'There's this blue carved stone, for instance.'

'No, I don't want that,' said Lucy-Ann. 'I really want to buy something for Philip. It's his birthday soon. Is there anything he would like? Don't let him see it – it's to keep for his birthday.'

'Well – what about this tiny carved ship?' said Lucian, holding out a miniature ship, exactly like some of the ships in the harbour. 'It isn't old, of course.'

Seeing the ship reminded Lucy-Ann of something. 'Oh! *I* know what I'd like to buy for him, Lucian. I've just thought. Something he badly wants.'

'What's that?' said Lucian.

'He wants a ship in a bottle,' said Lucy-Ann. 'I know it sounds a funny thing to ask for, but Philip says he always *has* wanted a ship in a bottle.'

'Well – I don't think I've ever seen one *here*,' said Lucian. 'It's not the kind of thing they sell. Wait a minute. I'll ask the johnny who's at the back of the shop. He'll know.'

He made his way through the masses of curious goods and disappeared behind a screen, where he could be heard talking to someone. He appeared again a minute later.

'No, they don't sell things like that here,' he said. 'But he says he knows where there is one, though it's rather a dirty old thing, and he thinks it's cracked.'

'Where is it?' asked Lucy-Ann. 'I could clean it up, if it isn't *too* badly cracked.'

'He says he saw it on a shelf in a house belonging to an old fisherman, not far from here,' said Lucian. 'I'll take you, if you like. Would Mrs Mannering mind?'

Mrs Mannering was with the ship's party, but she was keeping an eye on Lucian and his little company. Lucy-Ann thought she had better go and ask permission. They went out of the shop and found Mrs Mannering with the rest of the party having a cool fruit drink in a curious little courtyard overshadowed by an enormous tree.

'Aunt Allie – I want to give Philip a ship in a bottle for his birthday, and I've heard of one. Lucian says he'll take me to get it. May I go?' asked the little girl.

'Yes, but don't be long, Lucian,' said Mrs Mannering. 'It's not far, is it?'

'Oh no – just behind the market, that's all,' said Lucian, and set off with Lucy-Ann. They crossed the noisy market, falling over stray hens and getting in the way of a herd of goats. They came to a tall blank wall and went round it. On the other side was a sloping court yard, and round it were set several quaint little cottages made of stone.

Lucian went to one of them and shouted in at the open door. A croaking voice answered him. 'Want to come in?' he asked Lucy-Ann. 'It will be a bit gloomy, I expect.'

Lucy-Ann didn't really want to go in, but she thought it would be rude to refuse, so she stepped over a hen that was squatting on the step, and went into a small dark room that seemed to the girl to be full of laundry and the scents of smoke and cooking.

'There's the ship in a bottle. Look,' said Lucian, and he pointed to a stone shelf at the end of the room. There was a broken pot on it, an old bone – and the bottle! Lucy-Ann peered at the bottle to see if there was a ship inside. It was so sooty and dirty that she could not see through the glass.

Lucian said something to the old woman sitting on a stool, picked up the bottle and carried it to the door. He wiped it with his handkerchief, and held up the bottle for Lucy-Ann to see.

'There you are. You can *just* see the ship now. We'd have to wash the bottle in soapy water before we got the dirt off. It's quite a good ship – nicely carved. And I should think Philip would like it if he really wants one, though I can't imagine why anyone should long for a ship in a bottle.'

'Oh, I can!' said Lucy-Ann, peering at the ship. 'I've often longed for things like this – you know, quite useless, but nice and unusual. I had a friend once who had a glass ball, and inside was a little snowman – and when you shook the ball a whole lot of snow rose up inside the ball and showered itself down over the snowman. I loved that. So I know why Philip wants this.'

'Well – shall I ask the old woman if she'll sell it?' asked Lucian. 'The bottle is dirty and cracked, so it's not worth much.'

'Yes – ask her. You know how much money I've got. I can spend all that,' said Lucy-Ann. Lucian went back into the cottage with the bottle, nearly falling over two clucking hens on the way. A loud argument could be heard from inside. Lucy-Ann stayed out in the open air, listening but not understanding a word. She felt she could not bear to brave the dark inside the cottage again.

Lucian came out triumphant. He carried the bottle. 'Well, there you are. I've spent half your money. The old woman wanted the money badly, but she said she didn't know what her old grandad would think if he knew she'd sold a ship that had been in that bottle and in that family for years and years. However, as her grandad must have died long ago I don't expect he'll mind. Here you are.'

'Oh, thank you, Lucian,' said Lucy-Ann gratefully. 'I'll get a bit of paper and wrap it up. I do, do hope Philip will like it. It's an exciting present, isn't it?'

But it was going to be much, much more exciting than Lucy-Ann imagined!

8

The ship in the bottle

Lucy-Ann managed to get some paper and wrap up the bottle and ship before Philip saw it. The others were curious to know what she had got, but she would not tell them.

'It's something breakable, because you're carrying it so carefully!' said Jack. When they got back to the ship and she and Dinah got into their cabin, Lucy-Ann unwrapped the bottle and showed it to her.

'What a dirty old thing!' said Dinah. 'What is it? You haven't spent your money on that, surely!'

'Half of it,' said Lucy-Ann. 'It's for Philip's birthday. He said he wanted one. It's a ship in a bottle.'

'Is it really? Gosh, so it is!' said Dinah, interested. 'Let's clean it up and see it properly. Isn't it a big one?'

They rubbed soap on a flannel and proceeded to clean up the bottle. Once the glass was clean the ship inside could be plainly seen. It was a beauty, quite big, intricately carved, with carefully made sails. In contrast to the bottle, it was clean and free from dust. The colours it had been painted with were still bright.

'Look at that!' said Lucy-Ann in delight. 'It must be a model of one of the old Greek ships. How did it get into the bottle, Dinah? Look, the neck of the bottle is small and narrow – nobody could possibly push that lovely little ship through the neck. It would be quite impossible.'

'I can't *imagine* how it got into the bottle,' said Dinah, puzzled too. 'But it's certainly inside. Won't Philip be pleased? I rather like it myself.'

'Oh, so do I. It's wizard,' said Lucy-Ann. She stood it on a shelf. The bottle had a flat side, and stood on this, the lovely little ship sailing along, as it seemed, in the middle of the bottle, all its sails set.

'What's the ship called?' said Dinah, peering at it. 'I can't tell, can you? The letters on it aren't like ours. They must be Greek.'

The ship in the bottle was duly given to Philip two days later on his birthday. He was thrilled. Lucy-Ann glowed with delight when she saw how pleased he was.

'But *where* did you get it? Why, it's the nicest one I've ever seen!' he said. 'Quite the nicest. Really beautifully made. I wonder how old it is. I'm glad it's such a nice big one too. Most of the ships in bottles I've seen are much smaller than this.'

Micky and Kiki came to look at the ship in the bottle. Micky saw the ship through the glass and tried to get hold of it. He couldn't, of course, because of the glass, and it puzzled him.

'Happy Christmas,' said Kiki to Philip every now and again. She had been taught to say 'Happy returns' but she kept mixing it with 'Happy Christmas,' which she said every few minutes.

'Thanks, old thing,' Philip said. 'Happy New Year to *you*!'

'Oh, don't muddle her any more,' said Dinah. 'Let's go and show Mother the ship in the bottle.'

They went up on deck and found Mrs Mannering. Her deckchair was next to Lucian's aunt's chair, which she found rather trying sometimes, as she didn't very much like the uncle.

'Look, Mother – see what Lucy-Ann's given me for my birthday – something I've always wanted,' said Philip.

It was admired, and then passed on to Lucian's aunt and uncle to see. Mr Eppy looked at it carefully. He seemed puzzled.

'The ship is very old – really old,' he said. 'But the bottle is modern. The idea of a ship in a bottle is a comparatively recent one, of course. But the ship inside is far older – almost an antique! Very interesting.'

'It's got a name carved on it, very small,' said Lucy-Ann. 'I can't read it. Can you, Mr Eppy?'

He peered at it and spelt it out. 'Yes – A-N-D-R-A –

queer name for a ship! Never heard of one called that in Greek.'

'I've heard the name before,' said Lucy-Ann, and she tried to remember. 'Oh, yes – wasn't it the name of the girl in that lovely treasure story of Lucian's – the girl who didn't want to marry a one-eyed man? Well, we often call our ships by the names of girls or women – look at our big liners, *Queen Mary* and *Queen Elizabeth*. I don't see why a Greek ship shouldn't be called after a princess too.'

Mr Eppy wasn't listening. He wasn't at all interested in any of the children, not even in Lucian, his own nephew. He yawned and settled himself to sleep. Mrs Mannering nodded to the children to go. Micky and Kiki were rather tiresome when anyone wanted to sleep. Kiki's squawks and Micky's chatter and tricks didn't appeal to the grown-ups as much as they did to the children.

They took the ship in the bottle back to the cabin – this time to the boys' cabin. Philip decided to put it on the shelf opposite his bed, where he could see it. He was very pleased with it indeed. It was quaint and strange, and beautiful, and he had always wanted it. Now he had it.

'Be careful that monkey of yours doesn't tamper with it,' Jack warned him. 'He's very curious about the ship inside – keeps trying to touch it through the glass, and he gets quite annoyed when he can't.'

The *Viking Star* cruised from island to island. Time

did not seem to exist, and not one of the children had any idea of the days. It was all like a pleasant dream where, fortunately, the food tasted very real and very nice. In fact, as Jack said, if the food had not tasted jolly real he might honestly have thought that he *was* dreaming.

And then a squabble blew up between Micky and Kiki that broke up the dream in a strange way, and made things very real and earnest indeed from that time onwards.

It happened one evening. The boys had gone up to play deck tennis with the girls, and for once had left Micky and Kiki down below in their cabin. Micky was such a nuisance when they played deck tennis because he *would* fling himself after the rubber ring and, if he got it, tear up to the top of the nearest pole and sit there, chattering in glee.

So he had been relegated to the cabin that sunny evening with Kiki as company. Kiki was cross. She did not like being left behind. She sat on the porthole sill and sulked, making a horrible moaning noise that distressed Micky very much.

The monkey went to sit beside her, looking at her enquiringly, and putting out a sympathetic paw to stroke Kiki's feathers. Kiki growled like a dog and Micky retreated to the shelf, where he sat looking puzzled and sad.

He tried once more to comfort Kiki, by taking Jack's

toothbrush over to her and trying to brush her feathers with it, chuckling with delight. Kiki turned her back on him and finally put her head under her wing, which always puzzled and frightened Micky. He did not like her to have no head. He began to look for it cautiously, parting the parrot's feathers carefully and gently. Where had the head gone?

Kiki spoke from the depth of her feathers. 'Nit-wit, nit-wit, nit-wit, oh, I say! Grrrrrr! Wipe the door and shut your feet! God save the Queen.'

Micky left her in despair. He would wait till she grew her head again, and became the jolly parrot he knew. He put the toothbrush back into its mug and considered the sponge nearby. He picked it up and sucked some moisture out of it. He sponged his little face with it as he had seen Philip do. Then he got tired of that and darted back to the shelf again.

What could he do? He looked down at the shelf. On it was the ship in the bottle. Micky cautiously put his hand down to the bottle. Why couldn't he get that little thing inside? Why couldn't he get it and play with it? He put his head on one side and considered the ship inside.

He picked up the bottle and nursed it like a doll, crooning in his monkey language. Kiki took her head out of her wing and looked round at him. When she saw him nursing the bottle she was jealous and cross.

'Shut the door, shut the door, naughty boy,' she scolded. 'Where's your hanky, pop goes the weasel!'

Micky did not understand a word, and it would not have made any difference if he had. He shook the bottle hard. Kiki raised her crest and scolded again.

'Naughty, naughty! Bad boy! Pop-pop-pop!'

Micky chattered at her, and would not put the bottle down. Kiki flew across to the shelf and gave the surprised monkey a hard peck. He gave an anguished howl and flung the bottle away from him, nursing his bleeding arm.

The bottle fell to the floor with a crash, and broke in half. The little ship inside was shaken loose from its base and fell over on its side. Micky saw it and leapt down to it. Here was that thing inside the bottle at last! He picked it up and retired under the bed in silence.

Kiki was shocked by the noise of the bottle falling and breaking. She knew it was a bad thing to happen. She made a noise like a motor mower, and then relapsed into silence. What would Philip say?

Five minutes later the two boys came clattering into the cabin to wash and put on clean things for dinner. The first thing they saw was the broken bottle on the floor. Philip looked at it in horror.

'Look! It's smashed! Either Kiki or Micky must have done it!'

'Where's the ship?' said Jack, looking all round. It was nowhere to be seen. It was not till they hauled Micky out from underneath the bed that they got the ship. He had

73

not harmed it at all. He got three hard smacks, and Kiki got three hard taps on her beak.

'My beautiful present!' groaned Philip, looking at the little carved ship. 'Look, isn't it a beauty, Jack? You can see it better now it's out of the bottle.'

Jack looked at it and pulled at a tiny knob in one side. 'What's this?' he said. To his great surprise the knob came out and he could look inside the ship.

'It's hollow inside,' he said. 'And there's something there, Philip – looks like paper or parchment. I say – what can it be?'

Philip suddenly felt excited. 'Parchment? Then it must be an old document! And why should it be hidden inside the ship? Only because it contains a secret! I say, this is super. Goodness knows what the document is!'

'Let's probe it out and see,' said Jack. 'Look – this little section of the ship can be moved, now we've taken that knob out – and we'll just about have room to get out the parchment.'

'Be careful! It may fall to pieces if it's very old,' Philip warned him. Jack removed the loose section of the ship and put it beside the knob. Then, very carefully, he began to try and probe out the parchment. But he was excited and his hands trembled too much.

Then the gong went to say that dinner was ready. 'We can't go,' groaned Jack. 'We *must* find out what this is!'

'Look out – you're tearing it,' said Philip. 'Let's wait

till after dinner, Jack. We won't have time now. And I think the girls ought to be here to see all this.'

'Yes. You're right. We'll wait till after dinner,' said Jack with a sigh. 'Lock the whole thing up, Philip. We can't risk anything happening to the ship and its secret!'

So they locked the little ship up in a cupboard, and then, hot with excitement, went up to have their dinner. What a thrill! They could hardly wait to tell the girls!

The two girls could not imagine what was the matter with the boys that dinner time. Jack kept grinning quite idiotically at them, and Philip did his best to do a little whispering, to give the news.

Mrs Mannering frowned at him in surprise. 'Philip! You forget yourself. Say what you have to say out loud, please.'

That was just what Philip could not do, of course. 'Er – who won at deck tennis?' he said feebly.

'Well, really – I can't imagine why you had to say that in a *whisper*,' said Mrs Mannering. 'Don't be silly, Philip.'

'Sorry, Mother,' said Philip, not looking in the least sorry, but extraordinarily pleased. He simply could not help it. He kept thinking of the ship and its secret parchment. It was something really exciting, he was sure of it.

As soon as dinner was over the four children slipped away. When they got to a safe corner Jack clutched at the girls. 'Lucy-Ann! Dinah!'

'What *is* it?' said Dinah. 'You both acted like lunatics at dinner. What's up with you?'

'Shh! Listen! You know that ship in a bottle,' began Jack, but Philip interrupted him.

'No. Let me tell. Well, Micky and Kiki broke the bottle between them, the wretches, and when we got down into the cabin, there it was, smashed on the floor – and the ship was gone!'

'Where?' said Lucy-Ann, upset.

'Micky had it, under the bed. We got it and looked at it – and will you believe it, there was a knob that came out, and then we could remove another section of the ship – and inside there's a parchment document of some sort!'

'*No!*' cried the girls both together, thrilled to hear the news.

'It's true. You come down and see. Don't tell anyone though, especially Lucian. It's our own secret.'

They all tore down to the boys' cabin and nearly knocked over the steward, who had been turning down the beds.

'Sorry!' said Jack. 'Have you finished, steward?'

'Yes, I've finished – but what's all your hurry?' said the astonished steward. He got no answer. The door closed in his face, and he heard the latch being put across to lock it. Now what were those children up to?

Inside the cabin the light was switched on and the

cupboard unlocked. Philip took out the little carved ship. The others crowded round to look at it.

'See – you take out this knob – and that loosens this section of the side – and it comes right out,' said Philip. 'And now look – can you see the document neatly crammed inside? I'm sure it's parchment.'

The girls took a deep breath. 'Gosh – it's a thrill,' said Dinah. 'Get it out, quick!'

'We'll have to be careful not to tear it,' said Jack. 'Stand back a bit, you girls. You keep jogging my arm.'

How the boys managed to wheedle the closely folded paper out of the inside of the wooden ship was a miracle. Little by little they edged it out, until at last it was completely out, and the inside of the ship was empty.

'There we are!' said Jack triumphantly as he laid the yellow parchment carefully on the dressing table. 'Now to see what it is.'

With gentle, careful fingers Philip unfolded the parchment. It spread out into quite a big sheet. The children pored over it, thrilled.

'It's a map!'

'A plan of some kind!'

'I can't read the words. Blow, they must be in Greek or something!'

'What *is* it? It looks like some island or something!'

'Look at these marks – they must be the bearings of the compass – look, would that be north, south, east, west?'

'It's *two* maps, that's what it is. Look, this bit must show an island, I think – surely that's meant to be sea round it. And that bit is a plan – a plan of some building, I should think, with passages and things.'

The excited talk went on and on, each of the four children trying to press closer still to the map. Philip remembered that he had a magnifying glass and went to get it. Then they could see even better, and could make out a few strange words and marks too faded to see before.

'See this faint word here, at the left-hand side, right at the top,' said Lucy-Ann suddenly. 'Well, it looks exactly like the name on the ship, doesn't it? Let's compare them and see.'

They looked at both the words, first on the ship and then on the map. They certainly were the same.

'Well – Mr Eppy said the ship's name was *Andra* – and if the name on the map is the same, it must have something to do with an island or a person called Andra,' said Dinah.

There was a silence. Everyone was digesting this, and wondering if they dared to say what they thought it meant. No – it wasn't possible. It simply wasn't possible.

Lucy-Ann voiced their feelings first. She spoke in rather a breathless voice.

'Andra – the name of the girl who wouldn't marry the one-eyed prince. Do you suppose that one of the ships of treasure sent out and lost was called Andra in her honour? And do you suppose Andra was the name given to the search for the treasure – and that's why this ship and this map are marked Andra?'

'It can't be!' said Jack under his breath. 'It isn't possible that we have hit on the old plan that was lost – the copy of the older plan made hundreds of years ago! It just isn't possible.'

'It's probably a hoax,' said Philip, feeling perfectly certain that it wasn't.

'No – it can't be,' said Dinah. 'Mr Eppy, who knows about old things, told us the ship was old, didn't he? He was puzzled about it, because he said the ship was far older than the bottle.'

'Well, I'll tell you what *I* think,' said Jack slowly. 'I think this may be the plan – and I think probably that old Greek merchantman who copied the original one and died, hid it in this ship – which he may have carved himself.'

'Yes – and after he died his family may have kept it as a curio, not knowing what was inside it – and later on somebody else got the ship and thought it would be a very suitable one for putting inside a bottle,' finished Philip.

'But *how* did it get inside?' wondered Lucy-Ann. 'That's a real puzzle to me.'

'It's quite easy, really,' said Jack. 'The masts are hinged – they lie flat on the hull with threads tied to them. The ship's hull is slipped through the neck of the bottle –

then the threads tied to the mast are pulled, and up come mast and sails! The threads are drawn away and the bottle sealed with the fully rigged ship inside!'

'Gosh – how clever!' said Lucy-Ann. She looked at the ship again, and at the map lying beside it, old and yellowed.

'To think we are looking at a plan that was first drawn ages ago by a Greek admiral in charge of a fleet of treasure ships! And on this very map is shown where that treasure is still hidden – and we're the only people in the world that know the secret!'

It certainly was rather a tremendous thought. Silence fell on the four children. They looked at one another. Lucy-Ann spoke again, timidly.

'Jack! Philip! This won't be another adventure, will it?'

Nobody answered her. They were all thinking about the strange map. Jack voiced their thoughts.

'The thing is, as Lucy-Ann says – we may be the only ones in the *world* that know this secret – but it's all Greek to us! We can't read a word on the map; we don't even know the name of the island that's marked here. It's maddening.'

'We shall have to find out,' said Dinah.

'Oh yes – run round to various Greek people – Mr Eppy, for instance – and say, "Please will you decipher this strange document for us?" That's not a very bright idea, Dinah. Anyone who knows anything would see there was something worthwhile in this map – and it would disappear like a shot!'

'Oh dear – would it?' said Lucy-Ann. 'Do let's be careful of it, then.'

'I know what we could do to make sure nobody could possibly steal it and use it,' said Jack. 'We could cut it carefully into four pieces, and each one of us could have a bit – then if anyone tried to grab our bits he wouldn't be any better off – he'd only have a quarter of the plan, which wouldn't help him much!'

'Yes – that's a good idea,' said Philip. 'Though why we are imagining thieves and robbers like this I don't know!'

'Only because we've had a bit of experience in our other adventures,' said Dinah. 'We're getting to know how to handle them now!'

'And you know,' said Jack, still thinking of his plan, 'if we cut the map into four pieces, we could quite well go to *four* different people to ask them to decipher each quarter – without their seeing the other bits at all – so *they* wouldn't be any wiser, but *we* could fit their explanations together and get a complete picture of what the map means.'

'That's really a very clever idea, Jack,' said Philip, considering it. 'All the same – I vote we don't go to Mr Eppy about one of the bits.'

'I don't see why not,' said Jack. 'He won't be able to tell anything from one bit, and we certainly shan't say

81

we've got the rest. In fact, it wouldn't be a bad idea to go to him first – he'd be able to tell all right if it was a genuine document. If it isn't we shan't need to waste our time trailing round to find three other people to decipher the other bits.'

'Do you think he might guess what *we* guess – that this map is a plan of the Andra treasure hiding place?' asked Philip, still doubtful of the wisdom of asking Mr Eppy about the map.

'We won't give him the bit with the name "Andra" on,' said Jack. 'And we won't say a word about the other bits, or even where we found them. We'll just say we came across his bit in our explorations, but we don't know where. Lucy-Ann doesn't need to say a word. She's the only one who knows where the ship was bought – *we* don't. So we can truthfully look him in the eye, and say "No, sir – we haven't any idea where this bit of paper originally came from. It just – er – kind of appeared." '

'I hope he believes you,' said Dinah. 'He never seems to believe a word that Lucian says.'

'Oh, well – that nitwit,' said Jack.

'Lucian's really nicer than you think,' said Lucy-Ann. 'It was all because of him, don't forget, that I got this ship – I'd never have found the ship in the bottle if it hadn't been for him.'

'Well, he shall have a small share in the treasure if we find it,' said Jack generously.

'Oh – are we going to look for it, then?' said Lucy-

Ann. 'What about Aunt Allie? What will she say? And will the *Viking Star* mind us going to hunt for a treasure island?'

'Don't jump ahead, Lucy-Ann,' said Jack. 'How can we possibly settle anything in the way of future plans till we know what the map says? I imagine Aunt Allie will be as thrilled as we are when she hears about this.'

'Well, I don't,' said Lucy-Ann. 'I think she'll hate it. She'll take us all straight back home! She won't have us rushing about looking for islands and treasure, *I* know. She's had enough of that kind of thing with us.'

'We shan't tell her, then, till everything is settled – and, when it is, we'll send for old Bill,' declared Jack.

Lucy-Ann cheered up immediately. As long as Bill Cunningham was there, nothing would matter. The four sat down on the two beds, quite tired out with their exciting talk. They wished the electric fan would go twice as fast because they felt so hot. It whirred away, turning this way and that, a real blessing in the warm cabin.

A terrible noise, far louder than the electric fan made, came to their ears. They jumped.

'That's Kiki – making her express-engine screech,' said Jack. 'Come on – we'd better get her or we shall have the captain himself down to see what's up. My gracious, there she goes again. We've left her too long in the girls' cabin. Little wretch!'

The children hurried to the cabin next door, anxious

to stop Kiki before other passengers complained. Kiki was standing on the dressing table in front of the mirror, screeching at herself. Although she knew mirrors very well indeed, there were still times when she flew into a rage at seeing another parrot there, one that she could not peck.

'Stop it, Kiki, bad bird!' cried Jack. 'I'll tie your beak up, I will! Bad bird, naughty Polly!'

'Happy returns,' said Kiki, speaking to Philip and ignoring Jack. She made a sound like a cork being popped out of a bottle, and then another noise like the gurgling of a liquid being poured out.

'She wants a drink,' said Jack. 'Sorry, old thing. I forgot you'd be hot in here.' He filled a tooth-glass with water and Kiki sipped it thirstily. Micky came out for a drink too.

'We are awful,' said Philip. 'We forgot all about these two in our excitement. There's always water for them in our cabin, but there isn't any in the girls'. Poor Kiki, poor Micky!'

'Nit-wit,' said Kiki politely. She gave a realistic hiccup. 'Pardon! Micky, Kiki, Micky, Kiki, Micky, Ki—'

'That's enough,' said Jack. 'We don't think that's funny. Come along for a walk on deck. We'll all get some fresh air, and then sleep on our plans.'

They went up on deck with the parrot and the monkey. The other passengers smiled to see them. They liked the four children and their amusing pets. Kiki gave a hiccup every time she passed anyone, and immediately said 'Oh, I say! Pardon!' She knew that made people laugh, and she loved showing off.

It was cool on deck in the evening air. The children said very little because they were thinking such a lot. The bottle – the ship – the old map – quartering it – deciphering it – hunting, hunting, hunting for – Andra's treasure!

Down in their cabins that night they all found it very difficult to go to sleep. They tossed and turned, wishing they could get cool. Micky and Kiki were on the port-hole sill for coolness. The boys had it open always now, because neither of the pets showed any sign of wanting to go out of the big round opening.

Lucy-Ann lay thinking in her bed. She had the old familiar feeling of growing excitement and anticipation, mixed with a little dread. She knew that feeling! It was the one she got when an adventure was beginning. She called softly to Dinah.

'Dinah! Are you asleep? Listen – do you think we're beginning one of our adventures again? Do, do say we're not!'

'Well, if we are, whose fault will it be?' came back Dinah's voice, very wide awake. 'Who bought that ship?'

'I did,' said Lucy-Ann. 'Yes – if we plunge headlong into an adventure this time, it'll be all because *I* bought the little ship – the Ship of Adventure!'

9

The secret of the Ship of Adventure

When the morning came, the boys began to realize the difficulties in front of them concerning the strange document they had got hold of. The matter did not seem half so easy to tackle or a quarter so straightforward as they had imagined the night before.

Things the boys had pooh-poohed, such as Mrs Mannering's objections, suddenly seemed very awkward indeed. In fact the whole idea lost its rosy glow and seemed to recede into the realm of the impossible. It was very disappointing.

But when they got out the map again, which Philip had carefully put into an envelope and kept under his pillow all night long, the excitement of the night before swept over them once more. *Somehow* they must get the map deciphered, they must find out for certain if it was genuine – and then, who knew what might happen?

They made their plans. The map must be carefully cut into quarters. Each quarter must be placed in a small envelope, which in turn should be put into one a little larger. Each child must secrete his bit of the map either about his or her person or in the cabin.

That was the first thing to do. Then one of them must take his quarter to Mr Eppy and see what he said. Not the bit with the name of the island on, of course, but one of the other pieces.

'And Lucy-Ann mustn't come with us when we ask him,' said Philip. 'Because if he asks us straight out where we originally got the paper we can all say truthfully we don't know – but Lucy-Ann can't say that – and she'd blush or something and give the game away.'

'I should *not*,' said Lucy-Ann, who did not want to miss any of the excitement.

'You would. You're such a truthful person,' said Philip. 'Don't look like that, Lucy-Ann – it's a very nice thing to be, and we wouldn't have you any different. It's only that this is important, and it just might spoil things if you show there's something up.'

'All right,' said Lucy-Ann with a sigh. 'Perhaps you're right. I do wish Mr Eppy would take off his sunglasses sometimes – I just don't know what he's really like if I can't see his eyes.'

'I should think he's all right, except that he's a bit short-tempered,' said Jack. 'He's nice to his wife, and he's always very polite to Aunt Allie. Of course, he's pretty awful to Lucian – but then if *we* had poor old Rabbit for a nephew we'd be pretty awful to him too.'

'We are now, sometimes,' said Lucy-Ann. 'Like when we go on and on and on at him to have a swim in the ship's pool when we know he's scared stiff of the water.'

'It's only to see what excuse he'll think up each time,' said Jack. 'He's a marvel at excuses.'

'Well – what about this map – when shall we take it to Mr Eppy?' asked Philip. 'And if he says it's genuine, what do we do next? Is there anyone else on the ship we can ask about the next bit of the map?'

'Yes – there's the deck steward,' said Dinah. 'He's Greek. He could decipher it all right, I should think. And there's that little Greek woman who keeps the shop on the promenade deck – she'd be able to do a bit too, I expect.'

'Yes. We're getting on!' said Philip, pleased. 'Well – what about doing a bit of snipping?'

'I've got some very, very sharp scissors,' said Lucy-Ann. 'They're in my cabin. I'll go and get them. And I'll see what Micky and Kiki are doing there at the same time – up to some mischief, I expect!'

'Well, we couldn't have them here while we get out the map,' said Jack. 'Micky might quite well make a grab at it and throw it out of the porthole, like he did yesterday with the postcard I'd just written!'

'What a horrible thought!' said Dinah. She visualized their precious map sailing away out of the porthole and she got up to shut it. 'Just in *case*,' she said, and the boys laughed.

Lucy-Ann went to get her scissors. She was a long time coming back, and the others got impatient. 'What *is* she doing? She's been ages.'

When Lucy-Ann came back she had Kiki with her. 'I had to bring her,' she said. 'She had got Micky into a corner, and she was dancing in front of him from one leg to another – you know how she does when she's cross – and she was growling terrifically just like a dog. Poor Micky was scared stiff. I just had to stay and comfort him a bit.'

'What you mean is, you stayed and had a good game with them both,' grumbled Jack. 'Keeping us waiting all this time. Where are the scissors?'

'Blow! I left them behind after all!' said Lucy-Ann, and departed again in a hurry, looking rather red. She came back immediately, with the scissors in her hand. Kiki was now contentedly perched on her beloved Jack's shoulder, singing something that sounded like 'Humpty-Dumpty, three blind mice' over and over again in a very quiet little voice. She knew she had been naughty.

Jack took the scissors and, very carefully and solemnly, cut the precious document in half. The parchment crackled as he cut it. The others held their breath and watched.

Then Jack cut the halves into half again, and there, on the boys' dressing table, lay the four pieces – four exciting parts of a rare and unique document – if it was what the children imagined it to be!

'Now for small envelopes and then a bit larger ones,' said Dinah. She rummaged in the boys' writing cases and produced four fairly strong little envelopes. Each bit of the map was carefully slipped into one. Then four bigger envelopes were found, and the small envelopes were slipped into those. Good! The first step was taken.

'We can easily paste the four bits together once we have got all the pieces deciphered,' said Philip. 'Now – what's the best time to interview Mr Eppy – and exactly how shall we set about it?'

'It would be quite a good time now,' said Jack. 'He's usually up in his deckchair – and he'll probably be awake because it's not long after breakfast!'

'I say – are we to tell Lucian anything about this?' said Lucy-Ann.

'Don't be silly! Of *course* not!' said Jack. 'I wouldn't trust old Lucian with anything. His uncle has only got to bark a few words at him and he'd tell him everything he knew – and a lot more that he didn't, besides.'

It was decided that Jack's bit should be the one presented to Mr Eppy. It had not the name 'Andra' on it, neither had it the name of the island, so far as they could tell. It had one part of the island, with a few obscure hieroglyphics.

'What are hiero-something-or-other?' asked Lucy-Ann when Jack used the word. 'It sounds like a medicine or something!'

'Hieroglyphics? Well – these squiggly marks that we

don't understand,' said Jack. 'Marks that stand for words. Secret symbols, perhaps.'

'Secret symbols – it sounds thrilling,' said Lucy-Ann. 'Now – where shall I hide my bit?'

'*Not* in your writing case or anywhere obvious like that, Lucy-Ann,' said Philip. 'I know where I'm going to hide *mine*.'

'Where?' asked the others, and watched as Philip rose and went to his dressing table. It was fixed to the wall, of course – every bit of furniture in the cabins was fixed either to the wall or to the floor, so that it would not move if the ship rolled. Between the wall and the dressing table was a thin space, no more than a crack. Philip bent down and slid his envelope into this crack.

'There!' he said. 'No one will dust there – it's absolutely hidden between the bottom of the dressing table and the wall. Where will you put yours, Jack?'

'I'll keep it on me,' said Jack. 'My shorts have got a thin lining. I'll take out a few stitches so that I can slip my bit in. I'll pin it up afterwards. But I shan't hide mine yet, because I've got to show it to Mr Eppy.'

Dinah had thought of a really excellent place. She took the others to the cabin. Behind the electric fan was a panel of wood to which it was fixed. She slid her envelope neatly into the crack between the panel and the wall of the cabin. It hid it completely. She had had to turn off the fan to use the hiding place, of course – now she turned it on again, and the others voted her hiding place

as first class – no one would ever think there was anything hidden behind an electric fan that whirred round
and round all day and night!

'Good for you!' said Jack. 'Now what about Lucy-
Ann?'

'Think of somewhere that Micky can't get at,' warned
Philip. 'He's watching you. He can't get Dinah's piece
because he's afraid of the fan. He'd never dare to explore
behind it!'

'Could I slip it under the carpet?' said Lucy-Ann.

'No,' said Jack. 'The stewardess might feel it there
when she was doing the carpet and get it out.'

'Well – I know – what about at the back of a drawer
space?' said Lucy-Ann. She pulled out one of the drawers in her dressing table and set it on the floor. She got a
drawing pin from her pencil box and pinned the precious envelope to the very back of the drawer-space.

'There!' she said. 'No one can possibly see it's there
unless they pull the drawer right out – and why should
they do that?'

'Yes. That's fine,' said Jack, and the others approved
too. 'Micky's not strong enough to pull the drawer out,
even if he wants to. Now, what about going and tackling
Mr Eppy?'

'Right. Lucy-Ann, you go up to the deck-tennis place
with Lucian whilst we talk to his uncle,' said Philip.
'Then you'll both be out of the way.'

Lucy-Ann went off to find Lucian. He was mooning

about by himself, wondering where they all were. He was delighted to see Lucy-Ann, and agreed at once to have a game with her. He liked her the best of the four – probably because he felt she didn't make fun of him as much as the others.

'Well, *they're* disposed of all right,' said Jack, watching them go up the steps to the sports deck. 'Come on. We'll make for the deckchairs. Kiki, do decide which of my shoulders you want to sit on – this flapping to and fro is most uncomfortable!'

'I wish you'd have Micky for an hour or two,' groaned Philip. 'He's like a hot-water bottle by my right ear this morning.'

The passengers watched the three children with their parrot and monkey as they passed by. They had got used to them by now, and enjoyed the antics of the two pets. Mrs Mannering was on the watch for them.

'I wondered where you'd got to,' she said. 'Where's Lucy-Ann?'

'Playing with Lucian,' said Jack. He sat down by Mrs Mannering. Mrs Eppy and her husband were the other side of her. Jack spoke loudly so that his voice would carry well.

'I've got an unusual thing here,' he said. 'An old, old document, I should think. Do you suppose Mr Eppy would be kind enough to look at it for me, Aunt Allie?'

'Well, ask him!' said Mrs Mannering. 'He's here.'

10

Hiding places

Philip and Dinah were sitting on the edge of the same deck chair together, next to Mrs Mannering's. Jack was on the foot-end of her chair, with his bit of paper. They all looked very innocent and unconcerned.

'I don't really like to bother Mr Eppy now,' said Jack. 'He's reading.'

Mrs Eppy heard. She tapped her husband on the arm. 'Paul,' she said. 'Jack wants to ask you something.'

Mr Eppy knew that perfectly well, but he had pretended not to hear. He looked up.

'Very well,' he said grudgingly. 'What is it?'

'Just some old bit of paper we found,' said Philip, joining in. 'Probably quite uninteresting. We can't understand anything on it, of course.'

'It mayn't be old at all,' said Jack, flipping his bit with his thumb.

'It *looks* old,' said Mrs Mannering, getting interested. 'Where did you get it?'

'I don't really know – picked it up somewhere on one of the islands we visited,' said Jack. 'Do you know exactly where, Dinah?'

'No,' said Dinah truthfully. 'I've no idea.'

'Nor have I,' said Philip.

'Pass it over,' said Mr Eppy, sounding rather bored. His wife passed him the piece of parchment. He took it and glanced at it, meaning to pass it back with a scornful remark. What did these children know about old things? Nothing! It was probably a bit of an old letter, blown about by the wind, that they had picked up in the street. Or maybe they had bought something and this was part of the paper it was wrapped in. Mr Eppy looked at it and opened his mouth to say something contemptuous.

But he did not say a word. He went on looking and looking at the paper. Finally he took his dark glasses off and looked at it without them.

'Er – is it genuinely old, sir?' asked Jack at last, not able to wait any longer.

Mr Eppy did not answer. He was feeling in his pocket for something. He took out a little black case and undid it. Inside was a strong magnifying glass set in an eyepiece that could be screwed into the eye – something like watch repairers wear when repairing watches. Mr Eppy screwed the glass into his eye like an enormous monocle, and once more bent over Jack's piece of parchment.

He looked for a very long time. The children waited,

almost breathless. Why didn't he speak? Why was he such ages? It was mean of him!

At last Mr Eppy took the eyepiece out of his eye and looked at the children. They got a shock because they had never seen his eyes without dark glasses before. He had not nice eyes at all! They were decidedly cold. One was blue and the other was dark brown. Dinah felt a little shiver down her back. How very, very peculiar! She couldn't help staring at him, looking first at one dark-blue eye and then at the other dark-brown one. Was one false? No – how silly! – he would have eyes that matched if one was false.

'Well,' said Mr Eppy, and paused as if he was thinking what was best to say. 'It's – er – quite interesting. Er . . .'

'But is it genuinely *old*, Mr Eppy?' insisted Jack. 'That's what we want to know.'

'The parchment isn't all here,' said Mr Eppy, and his eyes glanced from one to the other of the children. 'This is only a piece of it. And judging by the *edges* of the parchment it has been recently cut. Rather odd that, don't you think so?'

This was most unexpected. Jack answered at once, feeling that there must be no pause which might give them away.

'Gosh – how very strange! Well, I suppose we've just got hold of *one* bit, sir. Er – I wonder who's got the rest of it.'

'So do I,' said Mr Eppy, looking at Jack and swinging his eyepiece to and fro on his finger. 'I should be very, very interested to know.'

'Why, sir?' asked Philip, looking perfectly innocent, much to Dinah's admiration.

'Well – I can't tell much from this one piece,' said Mr Eppy. 'It would be a help to have the rest.'

'What *can* you tell, Mr Eppy?' asked Dinah.

He looked at her with his odd eyes. 'I can tell that it shows part of an island,' he said. 'An interesting island – with some secret on it. I could perhaps tell what the *whole* secret is if I had the other bit of the parchment.'

'What a pity you haven't got it, sir,' said Jack, holding out his hand for his piece.

'*Where* did you say you found this?' said Mr Eppy, snapping out the question so suddenly that the children jumped.

'We didn't say – because we don't know,' said Jack, at once.

Mr Eppy frowned. He put his dark glasses on again, and became the familiar, rather puzzling man they knew, with his peculiar eyes completely hidden.

'I'll keep this parchment for a while,' he said, and actually took out a wallet to place it there.

'I'd rather you didn't, sir, if you don't mind,' said Jack. 'I'm going to take it home – er – for the school museum – if it's genuinely old and all that.'

'Yes, it's genuine,' said Mr Eppy dryly. 'I'll buy it off you. I'm interested in old things, as you know.'

'We don't want to sell it, Mr Eppy,' said Jack, getting alarmed. 'It can't be worth anything, anyway. We want it as a curio.'

'Very well. But I should like to borrow it for a while,' said Mr Eppy, and he calmly slipped the parchment into his wallet, and put the wallet into his pocket. Then he picked up his book and began to read.

Jack looked at the others in dismay. He was angry and crestfallen – but what was he to do? He could not snatch Mr Eppy's wallet and grab his piece of parchment from it. And if he kicked up a terrific fuss, Mrs Mannering would be angry, and Mr Eppy would get suspicious – if he was not suspicious already!

Philip and Dinah were dumbfounded. The cheek of it – taking their parchment like that! Would he give it back? They wished they had taken a tracing of it. If only they had! Now they might never get back their treasured bit of parchment.

They got up and went, feeling that they must talk about it. Mr Eppy took no notice of their going. Jack did not dare to say anything more to him, but he glowered at Lucian's uncle as if he could tear his wallet out of him.

They went to their cabin. 'Beast!' said Jack. 'Surly fellow! What sauce to pocket our parchment like that!'

'Hope we get it back,' said Dinah gloomily.

'There's one thing – we jolly well know it's old – and

98

genuine – and holds something most interesting to Mr Eppy,' said Philip, cheering up a little. 'We do know that. He was quite knocked out when he first looked at it – even had to get that eyepiece arrangement out. I bet he knows it may be part of a treasure plan.'

'I don't think, somehow, it was a very good idea to take it to Mr Eppy,' said Dinah. 'There may be markings on it that tell a man like that – who knows about old things – far more than they would tell anyone else.'

'I hope he doesn't guess we've got the other bits,' said Jack.

'He does,' said Philip. 'I bet he does.'

Lucy-Ann came bursting into the cabin. 'Hello!' she said. 'How did you get on? I had to stop playing with Lucian because that uncle of his came up and called him. He took him off somewhere.'

'He did, did he?' said Jack. 'I suppose he's going to ask him what *he* knows, then. Good thing he knows nothing!'

'What happened?' said Lucy-Ann. 'You all look rather down in the mouth. Wasn't it genuinely old?'

'Yes. But Mr Eppy has taken it and put it into his wallet,' said Jack. 'And I bet we don't get it back!'

Lucy-Ann was horrified. 'But why did you let him take it, you *idiot!*'

'Well, what would *you* have done? Knocked him off his deckchair, grabbed his wallet and run off with it?' demanded Jack, going through a performance of knocking somebody down and grabbing something. Kiki was astonished and rose into the air in fright, squawking. She settled on top of the cupboard in alarm. Jack took no notice of her. He was really crestfallen at what had happened – after all their wonderful, careful, clever plans too!

'We'll just have to hope he gives it back, that's all,' said Philip. 'And if he does, it will probably mean he's got a very nice copy of it!'

'We'll have to find out what he has said to Lucian,' said Jack. 'He'll probably tell him to try and pump us about this bit of parchment – and find out if we have the other bits – and where we got the thing from – and when – and where the rest of the plan is.'

'Yes. And we'll make up a perfectly marvellous tale and stuff him up like anything!' said Dinah, her eyes sparkling. 'Come on – let's think of one! If Mr Eppy's up to some game, we'll be up to one too. Now – what shall we say if Lucian pumps us?'

'Well, we said *we* didn't know much about it, so perhaps we'd better pretend that Lucy-Ann knows *all* about it,' said Jack, looking more cheerful as he considered the idea of pulling Lucian's leg, and perhaps Mr Eppy's as well.

'Oh dear,' said Lucy-Ann in alarm. 'Have I got to tell a whole lot of fairy tales to Lucian?'

'No. We'll do that for you,' said Jack with a grin.

'Now then – let's think. How shall we say that Lucy-Ann got hold of that parchment?'

'She was standing on the sports deck one day,' began Dinah, 'and she was feeding the gulls that live round about these islands.'

'And a great big gull came up with something in his beak,' went on Philip. 'He flew round Lucy-Ann's head, and . . .'

'Dropped a paper at her feet when he swooped down for bread,' said Jack. 'She picked it up and showed it to us – and we thought, aha, only a very clever man like dear Mr Eppy could decipher this strange document handed over by a generous gull . . .'

'And so we took it to show him,' finished Dinah. She giggled. 'It's too silly for words. Lucian will never swallow that.'

'He will. But his uncle won't!' grinned Philip. 'Serve him right. He'll expect to get the goods from Lucian when he's pumped us – and he'll find he's got rubbish!'

'Well, don't make *me* say it,' said Lucy-Ann. 'I'd go scarlet the whole time.'

'Listen – isn't that Lucian now?' said Jack. 'You go off, Lucy-Ann. Look, take this book, and say you're taking it to Aunt Allie. Go on. That will get you out of the way. It *is* Lucian. I know his idiotic humming.'

Lucy-Ann snatched a book and went to the door. It opened as she got there, and Lucian's rabbit face came round it.

'Hello, hello!' he said. 'Can I come in?'

'Yes, do,' said Lucy-Ann, squeezing by him. 'I'm taking this book to Aunt Allie. But the others are here. They'll *love* to see you.'

11

Lucian in trouble

'Hello, Lucian,' said Jack. 'Come in. Have a sweet.'

'Oh, thanks,' said Lucian, and sat himself down on the bed. He took a large piece of peanut crunch out of the tin Jack offered him. 'I say – this is jolly good stuff.'

'Like a game of deck tennis?' asked Philip.

'Er – well – actually I only like playing with Lucy-Ann,' said Lucian, who was so very bad at the game that even little Lucy-Ann sometimes beat him hollow. 'Can't give you others much of a game, you know. I say – my uncle's been telling me about that bit of parchment you showed him.'

'Has he? What did he say?'said Jack.

'Well, he thinks it may be the genuine goods, all right – but he can't tell without the other piece or pieces,' said Lucian, munching away. 'Oh, I say – look at that monkey. He's taken an enormous piece of nut crunch!'

'Yes – almost as big as your bit!' said Dinah, who

noticed that Lucian invariably took the largest piece of crunch from the tin.

'Oh, I say – did I really take a big bit?' said Lucian. 'Have to watch myself! You never told me about that bit of parchment. Why didn't you? I'd have liked to see it.'

'Well – it isn't very important, is it?' said Philip. 'I mean – we never thought you'd be interested.'

'Oh, but I *am* – like anything!' said Lucian, crunching hard. Micky was crunching too, and Kiki was watching him balefully. She didn't like nut crunch, but she couldn't bear to see Micky enjoying his. 'You might tell me all about it, you really might. Where you got it, and – er – everything.'

'Didn't your uncle tell you where we got it?' asked Dinah innocently. Lucian looked surprised.

'Gosh, no,' he said. 'Did you tell him? Well, why on earth did he ask me to find out?'

He had given himself away properly. The others winked at one another. 'Well, perhaps we *didn't* tell him,' said Jack solemnly. 'Did we, or didn't we?'

'Didn't, did, didn't, did,' remarked Kiki, thinking it was time that someone took notice of her. But nobody did.

'It's a shame not to tell old Lucian,' said Dinah in a kind voice. Lucian beamed.

'Yes. After all, he's a friend of ours,' said Philip.

Lucian was so overcome by this remark that he swallowed a bit of nut crunch and choked. Kiki immediately had a choking fit too. She did that kind of thing remarkably well. Jack thumped Lucian on the back, whereupon Micky actually went to Kiki and thumped her too. The children roared with laughter, but Kiki was furious with Micky and chased him all over the cabin.

'Oh dear,' said Dinah, wiping tears of laughter away. 'Those creatures will be the death of me. Now – what were we talking about?'

'About me being a friend of yours, and so you'd tell me about that bit of parchment,' said Lucian promptly. 'Oh – may I really have another bit of crunch? I say, thanks awfully.'

He took a bit, remembering not to take the largest there this time.

'Oh yes,' said Jack. 'We were saying it was a shame not to tell old Lucian. Well, old chap, it happened to Lucy-Ann, actually. Let's see . . . er . . .'

'She was standing on the deck, ready to feed the gulls that fly over from the islands,' said Jack. Lucian nodded. He had often seen Lucy-Ann feeding them.

'And suddenly a very large gull flew round her head holding something in its beak,' went on Philip. 'That's right, isn't it, Jack?'

'Absolutely,' said Jack with a solemn face.

'And lo and behold – when the gull came down for its bread, it dropped the parchment at Lucy-Ann's feet!' said Dinah. 'What do you think of that, Lucian? That's right isn't it, Jack?'

'Oh, definitely,' said Jack in a firm voice.

Lucian stared. His mouth dropped open. 'Oh, I say!' he said. 'Isn't that amazing! I mean to say – whoever would have thought of that?'

As the three of them had thought of it quite easily, they did not answer. Dinah felt a dreadful urge to giggle and turned her face away. Lucian seemed quite overcome with the story.

'I mean – honestly, it's like a fairy tale or something, isn't it?' he said. 'That gull dropping it at Lucy-Ann's feet.'

The others agreed that it *was* exactly like a fairy tale. 'Most extraordinary,' said Lucian, getting up and swallowing the last of his nut crunch. 'Well, I must be off. Thanks awfully for telling me all this. Oh, I say – what's happened to the bottle that the ship was in? You've got the ship without the bottle now!'

'Yes. Micky and Kiki broke it between them,' said Jack. 'Little wretches! Still, it's a nice ship and doesn't need its bottle.'

Lucian went out. The others grinned at one another. What a leg his was to pull! Poor old Lucian – he just *asked* for his leg to be well and truly pulled!

'I can just see him spouting that all out to his disbelieving uncle,' said Jack. 'Come on – if I don't get up into the fresh air and have some exercise I shall expire. Let's find Lucy-Ann and have a game of quoits or something. It's too hot now for deck-tennis.'

They played games all the morning, and then went

down to lunch, feeling very hungry indeed. To their surprise Lucian did not appear at lunch. They wondered if he was ill. Mrs Mannering asked his aunt about him.

'No, he's not ill – just a touch of the sun I think,' said Lucian's aunt. 'He's lying down and keeping quiet.'

'I vote we go down to Lucian's cabin and see if he's all right,' said Jack. 'He's never minded the sun before.'

Down they went, and knocked quietly. There was no answer. Jack turned the handle and went in. Lucian was lying on his bed, his face in his pillow.

'Are you asleep, Lucian?' said Jack softly.

Lucian turned over abruptly. 'Oh – it's you,' he said. Jack saw that the boy's face was blotched and tear-stained.

'What's up?' he said. 'I say, can the others come in? They're outside.'

'Well – if they want to,' said Lucian, who obviously was not welcoming visitors but did not like to say so. All four children were soon in the cabin. Lucy-Ann was distressed when she saw Lucian's blotched face.

'What's the matter?' she said. 'Is your sunstroke very bad?'

'It isn't sunstroke,' said Lucian and, to the children's horror, his eyes began to fill with tears. 'It's my beastly, horrible uncle!' He buried his face in the pillow again to hide his tears.

'What's he been up to?' said Jack, not very sympathetically, because he thought it was too feeble for words for a boy of Lucian's age to behave like that.

'He called me all kinds of names,' said Lucian, sitting up again. 'He – he called me a nitwit – and a nincom-poop—'

'Poop!' said Kiki. 'Nit-wit!'

'Now don't *you* start,' said poor Lucian to the parrot. 'He said I was a born idiot and a fool and—'

'But *why*?' asked Lucy-Ann astonished.

'Well, I told him how Lucy-Ann got that silly bit of parchment,' Lucian told them. 'You know – just how you told me. I thought he'd be so pleased to think I'd found out what he wanted to know. But he wasn't.'

'Wasn't he? That was too bad,' said Philip, thinking that Lucian deserved his scolding for running straight to his uncle with the fairy tale they had made up – they had meant him to, of course, but what a tittle-tattler he was!

'I said to him, "A gull brought the parchment down to Lucy-Ann and laid it at her feet,"' related Lucian in a dramatic manner. 'And Uncle said "WHAT?" So I told him again.'

'And what did he say the next time?' asked Jack trying not to laugh.

'All the things I told you. He was very insulting and offensive,' said Lucian. 'After all, he believed all the other things I told him. I can't think why he didn't believe *that*.'

'What other things did you tell him?' asked Jack at once.

'Oh, nothing much. He just wanted to know if I'd

been shopping with any of you – and where – and all that. I told him I'd been shopping with Lucy-Ann – and how we'd found that old ship in a bottle for her. And he said, "Ah – of course – the *Andra*! The *Andra*!". Just like that. I tell you he was most peculiar altogether.'

The others listened to this in silence. Mr Eppy had certainly pumped Lucian to some purpose. He knew they had bought the ship and where – he remembered seeing the name when they asked him what it was – the *Andra*. He was putting two and two together. Probably he already guessed that the parchment had been found in the ship because that ass Lucian would be sure to have told him that the bottle was broken and the ship free of it.

'Did you tell your uncle the bottle was broken, that the ship was in?' asked Jack.

'Er – yes, I think I did,' said Lucian. 'I say – I haven't done anything wrong, have I? I mean – you don't mind my telling my uncle all this?'

'We didn't mind your telling him about the gull and the bit of paper in the least,' said Philip truthfully. 'I'm sorry your uncle is so disbelieving. It was wrong of him to call you names like that.'

'It was, wasn't it?' said Lucian plaintively. 'He's got no right to. He called *you* a few names too.'

'Well, don't repeat them,' said Jack. 'You really ought to learn to respect people's confidences, Lucian. I mean

– it just isn't *done* to go round repeating to somebody else the things you've been told, possibly in confidence.'

'Now *you're* angry with me too!' wailed Lucian. Jack got up in disgust. This kind of behaviour was too much for him altogether. He did not even feel sorry for Lucian for getting into trouble because of a cock-and-bull story that they had made up specially for him. Lucian just walked into trouble as fast as he could!

The others got up too. Only Lucy-Ann was sorry about Lucian. Still, even she was disgusted at his tears and self-pity – really, he ought to pull himself together.

They went out without a word, leaving Lucian feeling miserable, upset, angry – and very, very hungry!

'Come to our cabin for a minute,' said Jack. 'We ought to have a few words about all this. Mr Eppy is putting two and two together a bit too fast. What an idiot Lucian is! Why did he have to blab about that ship so much? We'd better put it in a safe place in case Mr Eppy borrows it as he did our parchment.'

They went into the boys' cabin, and Philip gave a cry that made them all jump. 'Look – he's borrowed it already! It's gone!'

12

The second piece of the map

It was true – the beautiful little carved ship was no longer in its place of honour on the shelf. It was gone.

The four children stared at one another in exasperation. Blow Mr Eppy! What right had he to 'borrow' things like this? Would he give it back?

'What's he borrowed it for, anyway?' wondered Dinah. 'If he goes so far as to suspect that we found the parchment there I still don't see why he should borrow it. He's got the parchment, anyway!'

'A *bit* of it, only – and he knows it,' corrected Jack. 'He probably thinks the rest of it is still in the little carved ship – either that we haven't noticed it, or that we have kept it there. And he's borrowed it to see.'

'Stolen it, you mean,' said Lucy-Ann scornfully. 'Horrid man! I think he's awful.'

'Shall I go and ask him if he's got it?' said Philip. He was feeling very angry – quite ready to beard any lion in its den!

The others considered this. 'Suppose he *didn't* take it?' said Jack. 'It would be jolly awkward, accusing him of it.'

'Who else would have taken it?' demanded Philip. 'Nobody!'

'Look – let's go and have a swim in the pool and forget it for a bit,' said Dinah. 'If you still feel like bearding the lion afterwards, you can go. It's so awfully hot. I'd love a swim.'

'All right,' said Philip reluctantly. 'But I might not feel so keen on going after Mr Eppy afterwards.'

However, he was still of the same mind after his swim. The others couldn't help admiring him – they really thought it was a brave thing to do, to go and tackle Mr Eppy and accuse him of 'borrowing' their ship!

He went off to find Mr Eppy. He was not in his cabin. He was not in his deckchair. Where could he be? Philip began to hunt over the ship for him, determined to find him. He saw him at last coming out of the radio office.

'Mr Eppy,' said Philip, marching boldly up to him. 'What have you done with our ship?'

Mr Eppy stopped. Philip wished to goodness he did not wear those dark glasses. He had no idea if Mr Eppy was surprised, angry or what.

He soon knew. Mr Eppy spoke in a very snappy voice indeed. 'What do you mean, boy? What ship do you speak of?'

'The little carved ship we showed you – the one in the bottle – called *Andra*,' said Philip, wishing more than ever that he could see Mr Eppy's eyes and read what was in them. 'What have you done with it?'

'I think you are mad,' said Mr Eppy coldly. 'Quite mad. As mad as Lucian, who comes to me with a fairy tale about a little girl, a gull and a piece of parchment. What nonsense, what fiddlesticks! And now you come to me with a question about a toy ship! You think I have taken it to float in my bath, perhaps?'

'*Did* you take it, Mr Eppy?' persisted Philip.

'No! And do not dare to insult me with your fairy tales and your crazy questions any more!' thundered Mr Eppy.

He strode off, his mouth very grim. Philip was a little shaken. Well – he had not got much change out of Mr Eppy, that was certain. Blow the man! Philip felt absolutely certain he had got the ship. He went down to meet the others in his cabin. They would be waiting for him there.

He opened the cabin door and went in. 'Well,' he said, 'it's no go. He says he hasn't got the ship – but I bet he has. I feel it in my bones!'

'Then your bones tell you wrong,' said Jack, and he pointed across the room to the shelf on the wall. 'Look there.'

Philip looked, and gasped. The little carved Ship of Adventure was back in its place again!

'Where was it?' he asked. 'Gosh, what an idiot I've made of myself, accusing Mr Eppy of having it! Where on earth *was* it?'

'We don't know,' answered Dinah. 'We all came in here a few minutes ago after we left you on your way to tackle Mr Eppy – and the first thing we saw was the ship!'

'There it was, on the shelf – just where we left it this morning,' said Lucy-Ann.

'Who put it back?' asked Philip.

'Aha – if we knew that, we'd know who took it,' said Jack. 'I still think it was Mr Eppy. If you remember, he came in to lunch *after* we did – he could easily have slipped down here and taken the ship then. And he could just as easily have put it back whilst we were having our swim. If he saw us in the pool, which is quite likely, he'd know that he had plenty of time to slip down here and replace it.'

'The knob's a bit loose,' said Dinah. 'We think he found how it worked all right, and removed that wooden section and examined the inside of the ship thoroughly.'

'I see. And when he found there was nothing there he generously brought it back!' said Philip. 'I don't like that man. He'll be hunting round all our cabins looking for our other bits of parchment, if we don't look out.'

Lucy-Ann felt alarmed. 'Oh, dear – will he find them, do you think?'

'He might,' admitted Philip. 'They seem jolly good

hiding places to us, but they probably would be easy enough for him to discover.'

'I say – are we going to get the other bits deciphered now?' said Dinah suddenly. 'You know, we thought we'd ask the little Greek woman who keeps the shop on the ship, and the deck steward. Suppose Mr Eppy gets to hear we've been showing other people more bits of parchment. He'll soon be after them.'

'Yes, that's a point,' said Jack. 'But if we don't get them deciphered, we're no better off than we were. Hidden treasure is no use to anyone if they don't know in the least where it is. Anyway, we don't even know if the plan *does* show hidden treasure – all we know is that it is a genuine old document, and that Mr Eppy is distinctly interested.'

'I think we could trust the little shopwoman not to say a word,' said Lucy-Ann. 'She's nice, and she likes us. If we told her it was a secret, wouldn't she keep it? After all, we've got to ask *some*body!'

They debated whether the shopwoman was trustable or not. They decided that on the whole she was.

'She said she'd show me some photographs of her children,' said Lucy-Ann. 'She's got three on some little island or other. She leaves them with her grandmother when she goes on the ship. Couldn't we all go and see the photographs, and then ask her about the parchment?'

'Trust Lucy-Ann to know everyone's life history,' grinned Philip. 'It beats me how she does it! She already knows the names of the second officer's children, and she knows everything about the stewardess's old mother and what illnesses she suffers from, and she even knows how many dogs the captain himself has kept during his whole life!'

'I *don't*,' said Lucy-Ann indignantly. 'I simply wouldn't *dare* to ask him about dogs. Anyway, he can't have had any on board ship.'

'I'm only pulling your leg, Lucy-Ann,' said Philip. 'Actually I think your idea of looking at the shopwoman's photos and then springing our parchment on her – or a bit of it – is a good one.'

'Let's go now, then,' said Lucy-Ann, looking at the clock. 'Everyone always has a sleep in the afternoon at this time – no one is ever in the shop. She'll be alone.'

They went off together. Philip had the idea of first finding out where Mr Eppy was – just in *case* he should be snooping round!

He came back and reported. 'He's asleep in his deck-chair on the promenade deck. His head's well back, and he's not reading or anything.'

'How do you know he's asleep?' demanded Jack. 'You can't tell if his eyes are open or shut behind those awful dark sunglasses.'

'Well – he *looked* asleep,' said Philip. 'Sort of limp and relaxed. Come on – we'll go to the shop now.'

They went to the little shop. The Greek woman who

kept it showed all her white teeth in a pleased smile when she saw the children with Kiki and Micky.

'Ah, Kiki, Micky, and what mischief have you done?' she asked, tickling the little monkey and poking Kiki in the chest. 'One, two, three, GO!'

Kiki immediately made a noise like a pistol shot, which was just what the little Greek woman meant her to do. She was quite familiar with Kiki's ways, and always roared with laughter when the parrot hiccuped, coughed or sneezed.

'Tell him to snizz,' she begged. 'I like when he snizzes.'

So Kiki obliged with a fine variety of 'snizzes', much to Micky's amazement. Then out came the photographs and the children were treated to a life history of each of her three little girls. Dinah thought that surely never in this world had there lived such children before – so sweet, so good, so loving, so religious, so incredibly beautiful – and so extraordinarily boring!

Then Jack thought it was *their* turn to talk. He nudged Philip, who at once brought out his piece of the map. 'Look,' he said to the shopwoman. 'Can you make head or tail of this for us? It's an old, old document we found. What does it say – and what does it show?'

The Greek woman looked at it sharply with her bright black eyes. 'It is a plan of some sort,' she said. 'But you have not got the whole of it here – what a pity! It shows part of an island called Thamis or Themis, I cannot tell which. See, here is its name in Greek – but you will not understand the letters, of course. Your alphabet is different. Yes, it is part of an island, but where it is I do not know.'

'Can't you tell anything else from the map?' asked Dinah.

'There is something of importance on the island,' said the woman. 'Perhaps a temple? I do not know. There is a building marked here – or maybe it is meant to be a city. Again I do not know. I could tell you more if I had the whole of the map.'

The children had been so engrossed in all this that they had not heard the soft footsteps of someone coming. A shadow fell across them. They looked up and Lucy-Ann gave a gasp. It was Mr Eppy, his dark glasses hiding his eyes as usual.

'Ah – something interesting. Let me see,' said Mr Eppy coolly, and before anyone could stop him he had twisted the parchment out of the Greek woman's fingers and was looking at it himself!

Philip tried to twist it out of *his* fingers, but Mr Eppy was on his guard. He held it aloft and pretended to joke.

'He won't let Mr Eppy see! Bad boy!'

'Bad, naughty boy!' echoed Kiki at once. Micky, thinking it was a game of snatch, suddenly leapt up in the air and lunged out at the paper. He got it in his little paw, fell back to Philip's shoulder, and then, still with the parchment in his hand, leapt to the top of the shop and sat there, out of reach, chattering excitedly.

Mr Eppy knew when he was beaten. 'What a funny little creature!' he said in an amiable voice that managed to sound quite angry too. 'Well, well – we'll have a look at the parchment another time!'

And with that he left the dumbfounded children, walking off rapidly back to his deckchair.

13

Goodbye, Mr Eppy!

'*Well!*' said Dinah, finding her voice first. 'Of all the cheek! Philip, he *couldn't* have been asleep when you saw him in his chair! He must have seen you looking at him and guessed you were up to something – and looked about till he found us.'

'Blow him,' muttered Philip. 'Now he's seen *two* of the bits. He knows what the island is too because the name was on that second bit. That's an awful bit of bad luck.'

They left the surprised little shopwoman and went moodily up to the bow of the ship, glad to feel the wind in their faces. Micky had come down as soon as Mr Eppy had left them, and Philip had his bit of parchment back safe. But the damage was done – Mr Eppy had seen it!

'If there *is* anything in our idea, Mr Eppy has seen enough to cotton on to already,' said Jack gloomily. 'I can't say that we have been at all clever over this. Anything but.'

'Simply *given* our secret away,' said Dinah. 'We're losing our grip!'

'Anyway – I don't really see what we could have *done* about the treasure,' said Lucy-Ann suddenly. 'I mean – we can't possibly go hunting for it, even if we knew exactly where it was. So we might as well give it up, and if Mr Eppy wants to go hunting after it, let him!'

'Well, I must say you're very generous, giving up what might have been *our* treasure – and just saying Mr Eppy can have it!' said Jack, exasperated. 'All because you don't want an adventure again!'

'Oh, I say!' cried Kiki, and the children stopped talking at once. Kiki had given her usual signal for the approach of Lucian. Up he came, grinning amiably. He appeared to have completely forgotten his last meeting with them in his cabin, when he had been in tears. His face still looked a bit blotched, but otherwise he seemed very cheery.

'Hello!' he cried. 'Where on earth have you been the last half-hour? I've been looking for you everywhere. I say, look what Uncle's given me!'

He showed the children some pieces of Greek money. 'I expect he was sorry for going for me like that, don't you?' he chattered on. 'Anyway, he's in a very good temper now. Aunt can't understand it!'

The children could understand Mr Eppy's sudden good spirits very well indeed. They grinned wryly at one another. Mr Eppy had got what he wanted – or some part of what he wanted – and he was pleased. It struck Jack that Mr Eppy probably always got what he wanted, in one way or another. He wouldn't much care *which* way. He thought uneasily that they ought to find safer hiding places than the ones in the cabins for the remaining pieces of parchment.

He felt very gloomy. What was the use of bothering? *They* would never be able to do much about the treasure! How could they? Aunt Allie would not hear of it, he knew. And there would *have* to be some grown-up in charge. If only Bill had come on the trip with them!

An idea came into his head. 'I'm going off by myself for a little while,' he announced. 'See you later.' Off he went with Kiki, thinking about his idea. What about looking up the island Thamis or Themis, whichever it was, on a modern map and seeing if it was shown there? It would be interesting to see whereabouts it was. Why, it might be quite near where they were cruising!

He went down to the ship's little library with Kiki and asked for a good map of the islands. The librarian gave him one and looked disapprovingly at Kiki. He did not like parrots in his quiet library.

'Blow your nose,' Kiki advised him. 'Wipe your feet! How many times have I told you to shut the door? Pooh! Gah!'

The librarian said nothing at all, but looked down his nose. He had never in his life been spoken to like that – and by a parrot too! He was most irritated.

'One, two, three, GO!' said Kiki, and made the noise of a pistol going off. The librarian almost jumped out of his seat.

'Sorry about that,' said Jack hastily, afraid that the librarian would turn him out. He tapped Kiki on the beak. 'Manners, Kiki, manners. Shocking!'

'Shocking,' repeated Kiki in a mournful voice, and began to sniff in exactly the same way that the librarian did.

Jack pored over the map of the islands, forgetting all about Kiki in his interest. For a long time he could not see Thamis – and then there it was, before his eyes! It was not a large island, and was marked with what seemed to be a city or town just on the coast. One or two small marks seemed to indicate villages – but there was only the one town.

So that was where the legendary fleet of treasure ships went years and years ago! They put in at that city by the sea, sailing into the port at dead of night. How did they unload the treasure? Were the people there in on the secret? Where was it put? It must have been hidden remarkably well if no one had ever found it in all the years that had gone by.

Jack pored over the map, his imagination giving him picture after picture, and making him stirred up and excited. He gave a deep sigh, which Kiki immediately echoed. If only he could go to Thamis – to that city by the sea – if only he could just have a *look* at it!

But it would be Mr Eppy who would do that – Mr Eppy who knew all the islands by heart, and who could afford to hire ships to go from one to the other, exploring each one as he pleased. Jack folded up the map with another sigh. He put the whole idea away from him once and for all. You couldn't go on treasure hunts unless you were grown-up – his common sense told him that all the plans he and the others had made were just crazy dreams – lovely dreams, but quite impossible.

Jack strolled out of the library and up on deck. They were heading for another island. They were to go close by it so that the passengers might see the romantic coastline, but they were not calling there.

At least, so Jack had thought. As they came near he saw that he must have been wrong. The ship was either going into the port there, or people were going off in a motor boat that had come out to meet the ship. The ship's engines stopped at that moment, and Jack leaned over the side to watch the motor boat nose its way near.

It soon lay alongside the big ship, rising and falling gently on the waves. A ladder was shaken down the side of the *Viking Star*. Someone began to climb down, someone who waved back to others on the ship and called out in a foreign language.

And then Jack got a shock. The someone was *Mr Eppy*! He was calling goodbye to his wife and nephew. He climbed right down to the motor boat and jumped deftly to the deck. His big suitcase was lowered on a rope and swung down on the deck beside him. He looked up and waved again, his dark glasses showing clearly.

Jack scowled down angrily and miserably. Blow Mr Eppy, blow him! Jack felt sure he knew why he was leaving the boat. Mr Eppy knew enough to set things in motion for the grand Andra treasure hunt. He was going to Thamis. He would smell out the treasure that Jack and the others had happened on in that old map. It would be his.

And probably Jack would never even know what happened about it – never know if it was found, or what it was, or anything. It was like reading a tremendously exciting book halfway through, and then having the book taken away and not knowing the end of the story.

The motor boat chugged away from the ship. Mr Eppy and his sunglasses disappeared. Jack turned from the deck rail and went to find the others. He wondered if they knew about Mr Eppy.

He found them in the cabin. Micky had eaten something that disagreed with him and had been sick. They were looking after him anxiously. They had not even noticed that the engines of the ship had stopped and were now starting again.

'There!' Dinah was saying as Jack came into the cabin. 'He's all right now – aren't you, Micky? You shouldn't be so greedy.'

Jack came in looking so gloomy that everyone was startled. 'What's up?' said Philip at once.

'It's *all* up,' said Jack, sitting down on the nearest bed. 'Who do you think's gone off in a motor boat – suitcase and all?'

'Who?' asked everyone.

'Mr Eppy!' said Jack. 'Hotfoot after our treasure! He knows the island, he's guessed the Andra treasure may be there – and he's gone to set things going. At least, that's how *I* see it!'

'That's a blow,' said Philip. 'We've messed everything up properly. He certainly doesn't let grass grow under his feet,'

'We may as well give up all our grand ideas,' said Dinah. 'What a shame! I did feel so terribly thrilled.'

'I bet he had just been sending a radio message for a motor boat to take him off here when I met him coming out of the radio office,' said Philip, remembering. 'Just that first bit of parchment must have got him going. Now he's seen the second and he's certain!'

'It's bad luck,' said Lucy-Ann. 'We don't usually mess up things like this. Hello – who's that?'

'Oh, I say!' said Kiki at once – and sure enough the door opened, and in came Lucian with his everlasting cry. 'Oh, I say! What do you think's happened?'

'You've got rid of your uncle,' said Dinah at once. Lucian grinned.

'Yes. He's gone. Said he had had an urgent business

message and couldn't fool about cruising around with Auntie and me any longer. Gosh, I'm glad he's gone.'

'Yes, he's not a pleasant person,' said Jack. 'I'm glad he's not *my* uncle. Some of his little ways are not what you might call attractive.'

'They're *not*,' said Lucian, who felt he was quite free now to speak his mind about his uncle. 'Do you know – he wanted me to take your little carved ship to him and not say a word to you about it? What do you think of that?'

'Not much,' said Jack. '*Did* you take it?'

'Of course not!' said Lucian with such indignation that everyone felt he was telling the truth. 'What do you take me for?'

Nobody said what they took him for. They felt that it would be a pity to spoil his pleasure. Lucian beamed round at them.

'Now we can have a jolly good time, without my uncle, can't we?' he said.

'I can't say your uncle makes any difference to us one way or another,' said Jack. 'I don't want to talk about him any more. He's an unpleasant subject for discussion. There's the gong to dress for dinner, Lucian. You'd better go. You had no lunch and you must be ravenous.'

'I jolly well am,' said Lucian and went, looking quite delighted with life. The others, however, looked anything but delighted. In fact, they looked distinctly gloomy.

'Well – that's the end of what looked like a most promising adventure,' said Philip.

But he was wrong. It was not the end. It was really only the beginning!

14

Things begin to happen!

Things began to happen the very next day. The ship was cruising along as usual in a purple-blue sea, and the sun shone down from a sky spread with dazzling white clouds and patches of brilliant blue.

Gulls glided by, and all kinds of other seabirds bobbed on the water, or soared high above the ship. Everyone was peaceful in their deckchairs, reading or snoozing, waiting for the mid-morning drink of iced lemonade brought by the stewards. Even the children were lazing in their chairs, tired after their strenuous morning game at deck tennis.

Kiki sat on the back of Jack's chair, snoozing too. She had been chasing gulls, calling to them in a voice so like theirs that the poor things were completely bewildered. Now she was tired out. Micky was curled up in the shade of a lifeboat, fast asleep.

A small page-boy appeared, the one who ran messages

and fetched odds and ends for the passengers. He carried a long envelope on a salver.

He called out loudly as he went. 'Radiotelegram for Mrs Mannering, please. Radio for Mrs Mannering, please.'

Philip nudged his mother, and beckoned to the call-boy. Mrs Mannering looked up, startled to hear her name shouted out. The boy came up to her and presented the radiotelegram.

She tore it open, wondering who it was from. She read it out loud to the listening children.

Your aunt seriously ill and calling for you. Fly back if you can, and I'll take over the kids. Radio me, please.
Bill

There was a silence. 'Oh dear,' said Mrs Mannering. 'This *would* happen on a cruise. What shall I do? It's all very well for Bill to say "Fly back". But where from? And how can I leave you all?'

'Don't upset yourself, Mother,' said Philip. 'I'll see to things for you. I know the second officer very well and he'll tell me what you're to do.'

'As for us, you needn't worry at *all*,' said Jack. 'You know we're all right on the boat. You wouldn't want us all to fly back with you, surely!'

'Oh no. Of course not. Especially after I've paid such high fares for you all on this cruise,' said Mrs

Mannering, still looking worried. 'Oh dear – I do hate sudden things like this. I really do.'

'Mother dear, it's all right,' said Dinah. 'You can get a plane from the very next place we stop at if there is an airfield. You'll be in England tomorrow. And Bill will take over, as he said. He'll probably meet you at the airport when the plane lands there, see you safely on to your train, and then catch a plane to join us. He'll enjoy the rest of the trip. Maybe you'll be back too.'

'Oh no, I shan't – not if Aunt Polly has got one of her really bad turns,' said Mrs Mannering. 'She's been so good to me – and to you too – that I *must* stay with her till she's quite herself again. Oh, I do hate leaving you four by yourselves.'

Mrs Eppy could not help overhearing all this. She spoke to Mrs Mannering. 'I can keep an eye on the four for you till your friend comes, you know. After all, I have to look after Lucian, and he's much the same age. I shall be pleased to do what I can.'

'Well, that's good of you,' said Mrs Mannering, getting out of her deckchair, helped by Philip. 'I suppose it's idiotic of me to worry about them – they're all quite big now – but they do seem to get into such awful scrapes sometimes!'

She went off with Philip. He was very useful indeed. He found the second officer, and very soon he had worked out all the details with him. The ship would go out of her way a little and call at an island that had an airport. A radio message would be sent immediately so that a plane would be waiting. In no time at all Mrs Mannering would be back in England.

'We could wait at the island till your friend comes on *his* plane,' said the second officer after consulting with the captain. 'It would only mean altering our programme a very little – it is a very free-and-easy one, as you know. Now – do you want to radio instructions to Mr Cunningham so that he will know what time to meet your plane at the airport?'

It was amazing how easily everything was arranged after all. 'I was silly to get upset and flustered,' said Mrs Mannering to the children. 'Thanks to Philip it's all been arranged beautifully. I'll be away tomorrow, and Bill will arrive later – probably that evening. It's wonderful!'

The girls helped her to pack. The *Viking Star* steamed to a large island where there was a good airport. The children saw aeroplanes taking off as they came near, for the airport was on the coast.

A motor boat came out to take Mrs Mannering off. She kissed all the children goodbye. 'Now don't get into any scrapes,' she begged them. 'Be good. Keep away from danger and trouble. Give Bill my love and tell him if he leads you into anything I'll never, never forgive him!'

They waved goodbye as the motor boat chuffed away to the port. They watched it through their binoculars and saw Mrs Mannering getting out on to the jetty with a porter carrying her cases.

'She's got into a taxi,' announced Jack. 'Now she's off to the airport. She'll soon be away!'

Half an hour later an aeroplane took off from the airport on the coast and rose into the air. It flew towards the ship, circled it twice and made off to the west.

'That was Mother's plane,' said Philip. 'I think I even saw her waving. Well – safe journey to her! And now we must look out for old Bill.'

A curious silence fell on the children. They were all thinking the same thing, but nobody quite liked to say it. Jack cleared his throat.

'Er – you know – now that this has happened – er . . .' He stopped.

Everyone waited politely. 'Well, go on,' said Dinah.

'Er – I was just thinking,' said Jack, 'just thinking that now – well – with old Bill coming and all. Er . . .'

He stopped again. Dinah gave a little giggle. '*I'll* say it for you,' she said. 'It's what we've all been thinking, I know. Dear old Bill is coming – and we can tell him all about the map and the Andra treasure – and Mr Eppy. And maybe – *maybe*, he'll do something about it!'

'Gosh, yes,' said Jack. 'I didn't know how to put it without seeming a bit heartless, as Aunt Allie has only just gone. But things are a bit different now. Bill may think we *ought* to do something.'

'How – simply – super!' said Philip, drawing a deep breath. 'Just as we'd given up hope!'

'We couldn't *possibly* drag Mother into an adventure,' said Dinah. 'But Bill's different. I mean – he won't want us to plunge into an adventure, I know – but he may quite well think *he* ought to do something about it.'

'And we shall at least know what's happening,' said Jack. 'Won't it be grand to show him the little carved ship – and the map – and tell him everything! Good old Bill!'

Lucian came up with rather a solemn expression on his face. 'I say! I'm awfully sorry about all this. I do hope your mother arrives safely, Philip, and that her aunt will get better. I hope all this won't spoil the rest of the cruise for you. I am most awfully sorry.'

'Thanks,' said Philip. 'We shall get over it.'

'Oh, I say, I quite forgot to give you this,' went on Lucian. 'I'm so sorry. My uncle gave it to me before he left and said I was to hand it to you. I can't imagine what it is.'

Jack took it. He guessed what it was, and he was right. It was the piece of the plan that Mr Eppy had 'borrowed'. He had put it into a sealed envelope with a little note.

Thanks. Not very interesting after all.
P. Eppy

Jack laughed. 'Not very interesting, says he! I bet he's got a careful tracing of it. Much good may it do him!'

He went off to put it into its safe place – in the lining of his shorts. He was glad that Mr Eppy hadn't seen all the other pieces of the plan. Still, he probably did not need to. He might guess where the treasure was, if he knew the island. If so, it wouldn't be there long!

The day went by rather slowly. Mrs Eppy was rather annoying because she took very seriously her promise to look after the children. She hunted them out at meal-times, and even told the table steward to seat them at her table.

But Jack was not having that. 'No, Mrs Eppy,' he said firmly but politely. 'We expect our friend, Bill Cunningham, tonight – or at the latest, tomorrow morning. We will keep our own table and eat with him. Thank you all the same.'

Lucian was disappointed and sulked. He did not even smile when Kiki and Micky had a fight over a banana and ended by pulling it in half.

After the evening meal the children went up on deck, hoping against hope that Bill would arrive that night. The second officer had had no message, so thought he probably *would* arrive.

'He would surely have radioed me if he was coming tomorrow,' he said. 'He knows we're holding the ship here for him. All the same, I'd go to bed if I were you kids – he may come in the middle of the night!'

They would not hear of going to bed! They sat up on deck and watched the sun go down in a blaze of gold. They saw the clouds turn rosy-pink. Then they watched night creeping over the sea from the east, and saw the water turn more and more purple, till at last they could hardly tell it from the sky. Then the stars came out brilliantly, and the water sparkled again.

Lucy-Ann was almost asleep in her deckchair when Jack nudged her. 'Wake up! There's a plane. It may be Bill's!' She was awake at once, and went to the deck rail with the others.

The plane went down to the airport landing ground. It must be Bill's! After about half an hour they heard a motor boat starting up its engine in the port.

'It's Bill coming out now!' cried Lucy-Ann in excitement. 'Dear old Bill!'

The motor boat came nearer and nearer. It stopped by the ship, and a ladder was thrown down. Someone began to climb up. Lucy-Ann could contain herself no longer.

'Bill!' she cried. 'Is it you, Bill? BILL!'

Up came a familiar voice. 'Ahoy, there! Bill it is!'

And Bill it was. He came climbing on to the deck, and the four children ran to him at once. They smothered him, hugged him, and were bear-hugged back.

'Dear Bill! Good old Bill! It's grand to see you. *Now* everything's fine.'

'Yes, everything's fine!' said Bill, swinging Lucy-Ann right off her feet. 'Gosh, it's good to see you all! *Now* we'll have some fun!'

15

Bill hears the tale

Bill was hungry and thirsty. The children, excited and happy, took him down to the lounge, where he ordered chicken-and-ham sandwiches and a drink for himself, and, for a treat, some sandwiches for the children.

'Though, let me tell you, you'll have awful dreams tonight, having a meal so late,' he warned them. 'So if you are chased by bears, fall out of aeroplanes or get shipwrecked in your sleep, don't blame *me*!'

'We shan't,' said Lucy-Ann. 'Anyway, now I know you're here, I shan't even *mind* having nightmares – you'll turn up in them to rescue me!'

The steward brought the meal, smiling. He had also brought a banana each for Micky and Kiki, on two separate plates. Kiki was very much impressed with the plates – it wasn't often *she* had a plate! She insisted on putting her banana back on her plate each time she had taken a bite, which amused the children immensely.

'Kiki's gone all polite, I see,' said Bill, taking an enormous bite of his sandwich. 'Gosh, this is good. I haven't had anything to eat for hours. Well, kids, how's things?'

'We've a lot to tell you, Bill,' said Jack. 'Jolly interesting too. We've happened on something very exciting.'

'You would, of course,' said Bill. 'But don't think you're dragging me into any hare-brained escapade this time! I've had enough of you and your adventures! I've come out for a nice, quiet, restful trip.'

Kiki gave a tremendous squawk and made him jump.

'Micky! You've taken Kiki's banana!' said Jack. 'Philip, smack him. There'll be a fight soon, if you don't. All right, Kiki, I'll get you another. Poor old thing, that's what your good manners brought you – you put your banana down politely on your plate after each bite – and Micky goes and takes it!'

'Nice little monkey,' said Bill, tickling Micky under the chin. 'Yours, I suppose, Philip. It beats me how you collect pets wherever you go. Let's see – you've had a fox cub, a lizard, a slow-worm, a snowy-white kid, two puffins, white rats, and now a monkey. Well, well – so long as you don't collect a hippopotamus or a flock of lions I don't mind!'

The children were bursting to tell him about the treasure plan, but they felt they ought to let him eat his sandwiches first. He told them how he had met Mrs Mannering at the airport in England, and had seen her safely off to her aunt. Then he had taken his own private aeroplane and set off.

'Alone?' asked Jack.

'No. With a friend of mine – Tim Curling – don't think you've met him,' said Bill. 'Don't you want all your sandwiches, Lucy-Ann? Right, I'll help myself. Yes, Tim came too, and I've left him with the plane. He's going to hire a motor boat and do a bit of cruising.'

'Oh! I wish we could too,' said Dinah.

'*Do* you?' said Bill in surprise. 'But I thought you liked being on this big, comfortable ship. You're used to rowing boats and sailing ships and motor boats – this big ship must be a real change.'

'Yes, it is. But – well, shall we tell you our news, Bill?' asked Jack eagerly.

Bill ate the last vestige of the sandwiches and finished his drink. He yawned a vast yawn and Kiki immediately did the same. 'I suppose it can't wait till morning, can it?' he said. Then he saw the disappointed faces of the children and laughed. 'Oh, all right. Out with it.'

'Fetch the little carved ship, Lucy-Ann,' said Jack. 'I've got the four bits of the map. Hurry. We'll wait till you come back before we begin.'

Lucy-Ann sped off. She came back very quickly, panting, with the little ship in her hands. Bill took it. 'What a beauty! This is valuable, you know. Where did you get it?'

Then out came the story of how Lucy-Ann had discovered the ship in the bottle, with Lucian, and had bought it for Philip's birthday. In low, excited tones, so that no one else could hear, the children told of the breaking of the bottle and the unexpected finding of the parchment inside the ship. Then Jack produced the parchment, still in its four quarters. Bill glanced at it with great interest. Then he stood up.

'Come on down to my cabin,' he said. 'I think it would be wiser to talk there. This is all rather extraordinary.'

Very pleased with Bill's reception of their tale, the children trooped down the stairs to the cabins. They all crowded into Bill's. They knew it well because it had been their mother's. They managed to squash themselves on to the bed, with Bill in the middle.

'Move Micky up a bit, will you?' said Bill. 'He keeps breathing down my neck. Now then – what's this map? It's very old, I can see that. Why is it in four pieces?'

They told him. They told him the old legend of the lost Andra treasure. They told him of Mr Eppy's strange behaviour. They told him of his departure and all that they feared.

Bill listened intently, asking one or two curt questions now and again. When they had finished he took out his pipe and began to stuff it very slowly with tobacco. The children waited. They knew that Bill was thinking hard. Their hearts beat fast. What did Bill think of their tale? Would he take it seriously? *Would he do something about it?*

'Well,' said Bill, putting his pipe into his mouth and

speaking out of one side whilst he hunted in his pocket for matches. 'Well – I think you've got something there – but I'm basing my feelings on Mr Eppy's behaviour, not on your map, which I don't know enough about to decipher. You've been very ingenious in trying to get it explained to you, and you've fitted various curious facts together very well – such as finding the name Andra on the little ship, and noticing it again on the map.'

'Yes – that was a bit of luck,' said Jack. 'You really *do* think the map is genuine, Bill? I mean – do you think there's any hope of its really showing where the old treasure is?'

'I can't say,' said Bill, puffing away at his pipe. 'Can't possibly say. I'd have to take the map to an expert, get it deciphered properly, find out all I can about the old Andra legend – it may be just a tale, you know – and see if there really is an island called Thamis, and what it's like.'

'There *is*,' said Jack triumphantly. 'I found it on a map.'

Bill began to laugh. 'I don't know how it is that you children always seem to happen on something extraordinary,' he said. 'Just when I thought we were in for a lovely, peaceful trip I shall have to go hunting about for an expert on old documents, and get him to translate Greek so old that it's probably impossible to read correctly. And if there's anything in it I suppose we'll have to see this island called Thamis.'

'Bill! Will you really?' cried Jack in delight, and Philip bounced up and down on the bed, nearly upsetting everybody. Dinah clutched Lucy-Ann, her eyes shining. They were all so pleased because Bill had not pooh-poohed the whole idea.

'We'd better get to bed now,' said Bill. 'It's very late. We'll talk about all this in the morning – but don't get excited! We can't possibly do more than give this map to an expert, and then maybe run over to Thamis and back if it's near enough, just to give it a look over. After all – we're on a cruise, you know.'

The children got up reluctantly. Bill went with them to their cabins. 'I'm going up on deck to smoke my pipe,' he said. 'Happy dreams!'

In the early morning Jack and Philip woke up with a jump. They sat up in bed. Light was just filtering through their porthole, and a curious noise was coming from far below them.

'It's the engines of the ship,' said Jack in relief. 'I wondered whatever in the world it was. What a weird noise they're making! What's happening?'

'They've stopped,' said Philip, after listening for a minute or two. 'No – there they go again – clank-clank-clank. They don't sound a bit right. They don't purr like they usually do. I hope nothing's wrong.'

'Now they've stopped again,' said Jack. 'Well – if there's any danger we shall hear the ship's siren hooting and hooting and the steward will come along and bang on our door.'

'Yes. And our life jackets are ready in the cupboard, so we've nothing to worry about,' said Philip, feeling sleepy again. 'It's nothing. Let's go to sleep.'

But in the morning they found that the ship was still not using her engines. She lay there on the purple-blue sea, rocking a little, with the airport island lying not more than a mile or two off.

'Funny!' said Jack, and dressed quickly. He banged on the girls' door as he went by with Philip. The two boys tore up on deck and found their friend, the second officer.

'What's up?' they asked him. 'Why have we stopped?'

'Mac's got trouble with his engines,' said the officer. 'Soon be all right, I expect.'

They saw Bill coming along. He had been up for some time, walking round the deck for exercise. They rushed to him, and he grinned. 'Hello! Ready for breakfast? I'm ravenous. Hello, Micky, hello, Kiki.'

'Micky-Kiki-Micky-Kiki, Micky-Ki . . .' began Kiki. Jack tapped her on the beak.

'That's enough. Take a bit of exercise. Go and chase the gulls!' But Kiki did not want to. She was bored with the gulls now. Besides, she wanted breakfast. Breakfast was nice on board ship because there was always grapefruit, and Kiki liked that. She loved the cherries on top of the grapefruit halves, and the children took it in turn to give her one.

When breakfast was over they took Bill all over the ship. They were not allowed down in the engine room because of the trouble with the engines. Mac was in a fearful temper, and had been up all night long working on them.

A message was put up on the ship's noticeboard that morning.

Owing to engine trouble, the *Viking Star* is putting back to port. Passengers will be notified further at six o'clock this evening.

With a curious clanking and labouring the *Viking Star* made her way slowly to the island with the airport. Motor boats came roaring out to meet her and find out what was wrong. In one of them was Bill's friend Tim. He was soon on board, and Bill introduced him to the children.

'Tim, here are the four children I've told you about. Be careful of them, or they'll pull you into a perilous adventure. That's the kind of children they are. Put them in the middle of an iceberg and they'll find an adventure somehow!'

The children liked Tim. He was younger than Bill, had a mop of unruly curly hair which the wind did what it liked with, and eyes as green as Lucy-Ann's. He had as many freckles as she and Jack had, and a most infectious laugh.

'You'd better come off in the motor boat with me, hadn't you?' he said to Bill. 'Come back to the island. It's interesting.'

'Right,' said Bill. 'We'll have the day together. Come on, you four – down the ladder with you!'

16

Bill makes a few enquiries

They had a wonderful day on the island. Tim hired a car and away they went to explore. They had lunch in a big town set in the centre of the island, a proper town with shops and buses and cinemas.

After lunch Bill disappeared. 'I've heard of an old chap who's a real expert at old documents,' he told the children. 'One of the greatest experts there are. It's a bit of luck. I'll go and see him. You've got the four bits of the map with you, haven't you, Jack?'

Jack nodded. The children had decided that it would be safer to bring them than leave them behind. He gave them to Bill in an envelope. 'I *do* hope the expert will say it's genuine,' he said earnestly. 'I say – shall we tell Tim?'

'You'd be quite safe to,' said Bill. 'Tim is all right! Whether he'll believe you or not is another matter!'

So, while Bill was gone, the children told Tim their secret. He was inclined to grin at first and laugh it all off as a tale. But they were so serious that he saw that they, at least, believed in it all. He tried to be serious too.

'Well, it's marvellous,' he said. '*I* believed in all these treasure tales when I was a kid too. Jolly nice of Bill to take it seriously and go off to have your map explained.'

The children saw that he did not really take their tale seriously, and they dropped the subject, polite but disappointed. A little doubt crept into Lucy-Ann's mind. *Was* it all a tale? No – surely Mr Eppy wouldn't have behaved so oddly if there had been nothing in it.

Bill was a long time gone. The children were tired of waiting, and Tim was just suggesting they should take a run in the car to a strange-shaped hill in the distance when he came back.

'Sorry to have been so long,' he said. 'I found the old boy – looks as if he'd come out of the fifteenth century, he's so old and dusty – and so slow I could have screamed. But he knew his stuff all right.'

'What did he say?' asked Jack, crimson with anticipation.

'It's genuine. No doubt of that at all,' said Bill, and everyone breathed loudly in relief. 'He doesn't know if it's a copy of any older map, or a fresh one made by a Greek sailor a hundred or so years ago – probably a mixture, he says. The island is Thamis. It is shown clearly on the map, and even if the name had not been there it could have been recognized by its shape – it's curiously formed at one end.'

'Yes. I noticed that,' said Philip. 'Go on, Bill!'

'The map is in two distinct parts,' went on Bill. 'One shows the island, and on it is marked a city or a port. He doesn't know the island himself so he can't tell. The other part shows this same city or port, and is apparently a guide or directions to some spot in the city where something valuable is placed. He says it isn't clear if this valuable thing is treasure or a temple or even a tomb – he only knows it was something of value to the person who first drew the map.'

The children were listening, all eyes and ears. This was marvellous!

'But – doesn't he think it's the Andra treasure?' asked Jack.

'He apparently doesn't know that tale very well – he says there are hundreds of old legends of pirates and treasure ships and kidnapping and so on – most of them untrue. He hadn't much to say about that. He is inclined to think it's a temple.'

'*I* think it's the Andra treasure,' said Lucy-Ann, her eyes shining. 'I really do!'

'I got him to re-draw the whole map for us with the Greek words in English – he speaks English extraordinarily well,' said Bill, and he spread out a nice new sheet of paper on his lap, drawn with fine lines and marked with words. The children pored over it, too thrilled to speak.

Yes – there was the old map re-drawn – put into English – the faded marks shown clearly. How simply wonderful! Even Tim was intensely interested, and almost began to believe in it.

Jack read some of the words out in a whisper. 'Labyrinth – Catacombs – Two-Fingers – Goddess – Bird – Bell – gosh, what does it all mean? Are the labyrinths and catacombs in this city or port? Was the treasure taken down them?'

'We don't know. All we know is that a way is shown here to a certain place in the city where a certain valuable thing can be found – if it hasn't already been found and taken away or destroyed,' said Bill. 'But you must remember that the original of this map is probably hundreds of years old – the way shown on this map possibly no longer exists. In fact, the probabilities are that it doesn't.'

'Oh, Bill – do you really believe that?' asked Dinah reproachfully.

'Well – to be perfectly honest, I do,' said Bill disappointingly. 'I think the map is genuine – no doubt about that at all – but I also think that as all this happened so long ago there's no hope of finding the secret way shown here. It would either have been built over, or destroyed, or even completely forgotten, so that there may not even be an entrance to the labyrinths or catacombs, whatever they are.'

'But Mr Eppy obviously thinks there's some hope,' said Philip.

'Oh, that reminds me – this old chap, the one I've been to see, knows Mr Eppy. He says he's a real crank about these things – quite dippy about them – and goes off on all sorts of hare-brained schemes,' said Bill. 'Buys and sells islands as if they were books or carpets or pictures! He admits that Mr Eppy knows a lot about the islands, and about the antiques that can be found in them – but he doesn't think that because he believes in the map, for instance, that necessarily means there is anything to get excited about. Rather the other way about, I gathered.'

'Blow!' said Jack. 'So there may be nothing in it after all. In fact, probably not.'

'In fact, probably not, as you say,' agreed Bill. 'All the same, if we had the chance, which we shan't have, of course, I wouldn't mind hiring a motor boat and chugging off to have a look at Thamis, wherever it is.'

'Oh, I do wish we *could*,' said Lucy-Ann. 'It would be lovely just to *see* it.'

'I could run you over there,' said Tim unexpectedly. 'That is, if it's not too far away.'

'No time,' said Bill, folding up the map. 'We've got to be back by six, as you know. Thanks all the same, Tim. Now, we'd better be off, I think.'

By the time they got to the port it was half-past five. The *Viking Star* had been piloted right in to the pier, and was lying there looking very white and beautiful, but with no sign of the bustle about her that usually meant she was soon sailing.

The gangway was down, and passengers were trooping along it. Lucian was among them with his aunt. They had not seen him all day, except in the distance, and then they had taken no notice of him, not wanting him to tag himself on to them now they had Bill. He waved to them and shouted.

'Oh, I say! Where have you been all day? My aunt wanted you to come with us and have lunch with one of my relations on the island.'

'Sorry! We had other plans!' called back Jack. 'See you some time.'

'Who's the boy?' enquired Bill. 'Oh – it's Lucian, I suppose, the nephew of your Mr Eppy. He must be a bit of a nuisance to you!'

'We can manage him all right,' said Philip. 'Look – here's the noticeboard. There's a big notice up. What does it say?'

The notice was printed in chalk on the big black noticeboard.

Passengers are regretfully informed that the *Viking Star* will have to remain in port for a day or two until damage to her engines is repaired. Passengers may remain on board if they wish, or stay in a hotel provided by the Company, or may use the motor boats which the said Company will provide for the use of any passengers wishing to explore this romantic part of the Aegean Sea. (Signed) L. Petersen, *Captain*

The same thought struck all four children at once. They turned to one another, their eyes shining.

'We could, couldn't we?' said Lucy-Ann, and the others understood at once. Jack nodded, his eyes bright. He slipped his arm through Bill's.

Bill looked round at the children. He smiled broadly, and then laughed out loud to see the four eager faces looking at him, all with the same question in them.

'Can we go to Thamis, after all – that's what you want to know, isn't it?' he said. 'Well, I don't see why not. It looks as if we'll be here a few days, and if the Company provides us with a motor boat, well, we'll agree to their kind proposal and off we'll go in one!'

'*Bill!* BILL! How marvellous!' cried everyone, and Jack and Philip began to thump one another on the back, and the girls squeezed Bill's arms till he yelled. Kiki and Micky flew off the boys' shoulders in a hurry and retired in surprised annoyance to the top of the noticeboard.

'Come on – stop this pantomime,' said Bill, still laughing to see the children's excitement. 'Let's get up on deck and make a few plans before we change into clean things for dinner. Get Micky, look – he's beginning to rub out the top part of the notice with his tail.'

They went up to a favourite corner on the promenade deck and sat down. 'It's too good to be true,' said Jack, delighted. 'We keep on thinking things are no good, we'll have to give them up – and then something happens and everything's all right.'

'Yes. We knew we couldn't do anything without Bill, and he wasn't here – and then he suddenly came,' said Lucy-Ann.

'And then we knew we still couldn't do anything because we'd have to go with the ship on her cruise,' said Dinah. 'And now she's held up, and we can go off by ourselves!'

'Extraordinary how you children get what you want,' said Bill. 'Now about this motor boat tomorrow. I rather think we'll hire one on our own. If we take one that the Company provides we'll have to go with some of the other passengers – and they certainly won't want to go to Thamis, wherever it is.'

'And we wouldn't want them to, either,' said Jack. 'No – let's have a boat of our own. Can Tim come too?'

'He's got other plans,' said Bill. 'But we'll tell him, just in case he'd like to come. Well – it certainly will be a thrill. I must find out this evening exactly where this Thamis is. I'll get hold of the second officer and ask him if there's a sailor on board who can tell me anything.

We'll have to find out the precise route or we might go cruising among these islands for weeks!'

'Oh, Bill – isn't it grand?' said Lucy-Ann. 'I can't wait for tomorrow. Jack, Philip – we're really going to see the treasure island after all! We really are!'

17

To Thamis at last!

Bill soon got all the information he wanted. 'That's the best of being grown-up,' said Dinah. 'Grown-ups always seem to be able to find out anything, and get things cut and dried in no time.'

'Yes – Bill's found out where Thamis is, has ferreted out a map of the route, and has even got the name of a Greek sailor who owns a motor boat and knows the way!' said Jack, in admiration.

'How did he find all that out?' asked Lucy-Ann.

'Got hold of a Greek sailor below decks, and found he had a brother who runs one of the motor boats,' said Philip.

It was the following morning. The children had had a big breakfast, and had been provided with enormous packets of food to take with them by the steward who looked after them so well at table.

'I've packed a whole grapefruit, two cherries and four

bananas for Master Micky and Miss Kiki,' he said with a twinkle in his eye. Lucy-Ann went off into giggles.

'Oh – it does sound funny to call them that! Miss Kiki! Kiki, did you hear that? Miss Kiki!'

'Misskiki, kickmissy, missmicky,' said Kiki and cackled loudly.

They all walked down the gangway to the pier. They found Tim waiting for them. He had heard the news.

'Hello, sir,' he said to Bill. 'Can I do anything for you today?'

'Well, we're going off to have a look at Thamis,' said Bill. 'I've hired a motor boat from a Greek who apparently knows the route. Like to come with us?'

'Well, if you've made your own plans, sir, I won't come today,' said Tim. 'I've got a chappy here who wants a spot of flying. Can I take the plane up?'

'Yes, of course,' said Bill.

'And if you fly over Thamis, wave to us,' said Jack.

'Right,' said Tim with a grin. 'I'll look it up and see where it is. Look out for us!'

He went off, and Bill turned to find the boat he had hired. A Greek man came up, with brilliant eyes and a shy smile. He saluted, and spoke in broken English.

'I'm Andros, sir, please. My brother, he say Mister want my boat. Mister, sir, she here.'

'Right. Thanks, Andros,' said Bill, and he looked at

the spick-and-span little boat lying alongside. 'Very nice boat. Now, you know the way to Thamis, don't you?'

'Thamis. Yes, Mister. But Thamis poor place. Andros take you find islands.'

'No, thanks. We want to go to Thamis,' said Bill firmly.

Andros seemed surprised at their wanting to go to Thamis. 'Poor island,' he said again. 'Visitors not go there, Mister, sir. I take you fine place.'

'Look here – don't you know the way to Thamis?' said Bill. 'Sounds as if you don't. Oh, you do. Then to Thamis, please, and let's get on with it.'

'Thamis, Mister, sir,' agreed little Andros. 'Yes, yes, Thamis. Old, old island, but nothing there now, Mister, sir.' He glanced with interest at the parrot and the monkey. 'They come too also?'

'Of course,' said Jack, stepping into the boat and helping the girls in. 'Come on, Bill, Mister, sir!'

'Mistersir, mistersir, mistersir,' screamed Kiki. 'Pop goes the weasel! Bang, pop, God save the Queen.'

Andros gaped at her open-mouthed. Micky leapt on to his shoulder and back to Philip's, chattering. He was excited. He even pulled Kiki's tail, a very silly thing to do because Kiki would now watch for a good chance to nip Micky's – and Micky had quite a long tail to nip!

Andros started up the engine. The motor boat nosed out of the little harbour, leaving behind the great *Viking Star*, beautiful but silent. Soon they were out on the open sea, skimming along, bobbing up and down on the white horses that reared themselves every now and again. The sun was hot but the wind was strong. The girls' hair streamed out straight, and they laughed in delight to feel so much wind in their faces. After the heat on the ship it was lovely.

'How far is Thamis?' asked Jack. Andros turned his curly head.

'Four hours, five hours,' he said.

'Do you go there much?' asked Bill.

'No, no, Mister, sir. Poor island. I go to Janos, the next one, where my sister lives,' said Andros. 'Thamis dead island, Mister, sir.'

'What does he mean?' wondered Jack. 'A poor dead island! Doesn't sound much of a place, does it?'

'Well, there must be some sort of port or town there,' said Philip. 'The one marked on the map. It looked quite a big one. There must be plenty of people living there, and that means shops and things. It can't be quite dead!'

It was a lovely journey to Thamis. The sea was choppy, and yet was full of glints and sparkles. The boat sped along like a live thing, the engine purring away. At twelve o'clock they all had a picnic lunch and blessed the steward who had packed them such a fine one.

'Five different sorts of sandwiches – four different kinds of cake, half a pound of sweet biscuits, rolls and butter and cheese and tomatoes – and the grapefruit, cherries and bananas for Kiki and Micky,' said Jack.

Lucy-Ann sat contentedly eating with the wind in her face. She looked very happy. The others looked at her and nudged one another. They waited. They knew exactly what she was going to say. She opened her mouth, and at once all the others chimed in together.

'You know, we always think food tastes *much* nicer when it's eaten out of doors!'

Lucy-Ann stared at them in surprise. 'How very peculiar! I was *just* about to say exactly the same thing,' she said.

The others chuckled. 'We knew you were,' said Philip. 'You always do say it, Lucy-Ann. We watched for you to open your mouth and begin, and we said it for you!'

'Idiots,' said Lucy-Ann and laughed. Andros laughed too. He liked these children and their funny pets. He had refused to share their food and was eating his own lunch. It was made up of black bread, some very strong-smelling cheese and a jug of some kind of drink.

Kiki and Micky ate their dinner solemnly together. Micky was not very pleased with the terrific breeze that blew every hair on his body backwards or forwards, depending on which way he sat. Nor was Kiki pleased when her feathers blew round her like an umbrella turning inside out. The two of them sat together in a little sheltered place sharing the grapefruit, the cherries and the bananas. Micky politely peeled a banana for Kiki and handed it to her.

'He skins it just like we do,' said Lucy-Ann. 'I always think he's so clever at that.'

'Clever,' said Andros, pointing to Micky. 'Good and clever.'

Micky unfortunately spoilt Andros's good opinion of him by throwing away the banana skin so carelessly that it landed on the sailor's head, hanging ridiculously over his right eye. Kiki gave one of her rich chuckles, and was just about to add her banana skin to Micky's when Jack took it away from her.

'Mistersir, mistersir, mister Pollysir,' squawked Kiki, trying to snatch it back.

The boat went on and on, occasionally passing other islands, one or two large ones, but most of them small. Finally Andros raised his hand and pointed to the east.

'Thamis,' he said. 'Mister, sir, Thamis.'

Everyone looked eagerly to where he pointed. They saw a small island, purple in the distance, rearing itself out of the waters as they sped nearer. Thamis! Was it really Thamis, the old island marked on the treasure map?

Eagerly the children leaned forward and watched it take shape as they raced nearer. Lucy-Ann's imagination began to work. Long, long ago, she thought, this is where the fleet of treasure ships stole up to in the night. Soon we shall see the city marked on the map – the treasure city!

'Perhaps,' she thought, 'one of the ships was called the

Andra like our own little Ship of Adventure. Perhaps it sailed into the very spot we're making for now. We're getting quite near. We shall see the city soon – the one marked on the map.'

'Is there a good harbour?' asked Bill, turning to Andros. The man looked surprised.

'Oh, no, Mister, sir. No harbour now. Only two places to land. I, Andros, know them both. I take you to old city port.'

'Good,' thought Jack. 'Now we shall soon be there – in the old city marked on the map. I hope it won't be *too* modern, like the towns we've seen on some of the islands. Ah – now we're getting in close.'

They were. They could see rocky beaches. The waves pounded on them. They looked for the town, and saw buildings coming down to the water's edge. It seemed strange that there was no proper harbour. City ports always had a harbour.

The boat ran in gently, Andros looking out for rocks and taking a course he seemed to know. He was making for a little channel that led inland.

The children fell silent as they neared the island. Their eyes were fixed on the city. It did not look right, somehow. Something was the matter with it. It looked – well – *dead*, Lucy-Ann thought.

Jack remembered his binoculars and put them to his eyes. He gave an exclamation. 'Gosh! Would you believe it!'

'*What?*' said everyone at once impatiently.

'It's all ruins,' said Jack, and he lowered the glasses and looked at the others. 'It's a *ruined* city! I never thought of that!'

'I, Andros, told that,' said the sailor. 'I tell you poor island, dead island. One farm, two farms, perhaps. City gone. Nobody there. All gone to other islands now.'

They nosed into the little channel. It was deep and calm. 'You get out and I wait?' enquired Andros. 'Not see much. All dead and poor this island. Yes, Mister, sir. I take you better places.'

'We'll get out, Andros,' said Bill. 'Bring the rest of the food, Jack. We may as well explore now we're here, and we'll picnic in the old ruins. They will be quite interesting, I expect.'

Not knowing quite what to think, the children leapt off the boat on to a ledge. They climbed up some old worn steps, and came into what must have been the main street of the ruined city. It was overgrown now and difficult to walk in. There were ruins everywhere. Bill looked at a few of them closely.

'These are hundreds of years old,' he said. 'I wonder what made the people leave Thamis and go elsewhere. I suppose the island couldn't keep them in food. What a place!'

'It's got such a weird deserted feeling about it that I feel I'm living hundreds of years ago,' said Lucy-Ann. 'I wish the city would come alive – be full of the long-ago people, walking and running here along the street, looking out of the old broken window-openings, going down to whatever harbour there was to see the ships!'

'Well, I hope the city *doesn't* come alive,' said Dinah. 'I'd be scared stiff. I don't like it much as it is.'

It was built on a steep hill, and the ruined buildings rose one above another, some just a wall or two, others a hollow shell, and still others looking fairly habitable until the children peeped inside and saw the holes in the roofs and the walls.

Almost at the top was an old ruined temple, one or two graceful arches still remaining. Its massive columns stood in a broken row, with one or two gulls perched on the jagged tops. Bill scraped aside some of the grass that grew on the floor of the temple, and pointed out lovely mosaic stones to the children.

'Bill, is there anything here at all that's on the map?' asked Jack. Somehow it was all so different from what he had imagined that the idea of hidden treasure now seemed ridiculous. Bill got out the re-drawn map.

'Look – this is where we came in with our boat, surely,' said Philip, pointing. 'It says "CREEK". Well, wouldn't you call that channel a creek? And look – the entrance or beginning of the way to the treasure is some-where near the creek.'

'Oh, Bill – let's go back and explore along there!' said Dinah.

Bill laughed. 'We've certainly got a bee in our bonnet about this! All right. Come on. It'll be on the way to the boat, anyway.'

'Just let's get to the top of the hill,' said Jack. 'We could see over the rest of the island then. It's not very large.'

'Right,' said Bill, and they climbed to the very top. They could see away over to the other side of the island, where the dark-blue sea was tipped with white horses. It was a bare, rocky place, but here and there were green patches, and small buildings could be seen.

'The farms Andros spoke of, I suppose,' said Bill. 'My word – he was certainly right when he called it poor and dead! It's not quite my idea of a treasure island!'

They turned to go down the hill on which the ruined city was built. They made their way carefully. Halfway down Lucy-Ann stopped and listened. 'I can hear something,' she said.

'So can I,' said Dinah. 'It's a bell ringing! Whatever can it be?'

18

A few surprises

It seemed so very unusual to hear a bell ringing in that dead and silent city that the little company felt really startled. The sound came nearer.

'Dong-dong-dong.' Kiki didn't like it either and crouched against Jack's cheek. Micky chattered quietly.

'Dong-dong-dong!'

'Something's coming round that corner,' said Jack suddenly. And something did.

It was a donkey, a little grey donkey with a big bell hanging from his neck! With him was a small boy, an imp of a boy, riding astride, with panniers each side of the donkey, great baskets that were full of something covered with white cloths.

'Good gracious!' said Dinah, and she sat down on a big stone, most relieved to see that it was just a donkey bell that had startled them all. 'I don't know *what* I thought was coming!'

'I suppose the boy's from one of the farms,' said Bill,

looking puzzled. 'But why has he come here? There is nobody living here.'

Then an even more surprising thing happened. The boy caught sight of the five people watching him and grinned a welcome. He leapt off the donkey, pointed to the pannier baskets and shouted out something that sounded unlike anything they had heard before, but which the children imagined must be Greek spoken in the local accent of Thamis. Then he brought the donkey right up to them and began to throw back the cloths that covered whatever was in the panniers.

'It's food,' said Bill in amazement. 'Bread – cheeses – meat. Gosh, he's unpacking the lot.'

The boy unpacked everything, chattering all the time. He evidently could not understand why nobody helped him, and addressed quite a few cutting remarks to the two boys, who, of course, could not make head or tail of them.

'Here, boy,' said Bill. 'What's all this?'

He pointed to the pile of food. The boy sent out another explanation, pointing to Bill and then pointing to the food.

'Anyone would think he had brought all this for *us*,' said Bill, exasperated. 'I can't understand it at all.'

The boy mounted his donkey again. He held out his hand to Bill, palm upwards. That was plain enough. He wanted money!

'Well, well – it beats me,' said Bill astounded. 'A very

fine welcome to Thamis, I must say – but most unexpected. We don't want the food, sonny. WE DONT WANT IT. TAKE IT BACK!'

No amount of shouting could make the boy understand. He got very angry, and tapped his palm smartly to make Bill understand he wanted money. In the end Bill tipped a handful of coins into his hand. He counted them carefully, nodded his head, grinned brilliantly, and then very unexpectedly spat at Micky. Micky spat back, and Kiki growled like a dog.

The donkey backed away from Kiki and began to bray. 'Eee-yore! Eee-eee-yore!'

Kiki was extremely startled, but she soon recovered, and produced a very good bray herself. The boy gave a yelp of surprise, kicked his donkey hard with both his bare heels and galloped away round the corner, the donkey's bell ringing hard. 'Dong-dong-dong-dong-dong!'

Bill sat down and scratched his head. 'Well, what do you make of *that*?' he said. 'A present of some very fine country food, sent by somebody we don't know, who can't possibly have known we were here.'

'It's a puzzle,' said Jack. 'I wouldn't mind one of those rolls.'

They all had one. They were very good. They sat and munched them, wondering about the boy. They could not make head or tail of his appearance.

'What are we going to do with this food?' said Philip.

'It won't keep if it's left out in the sun. It seems an awful waste of good food to leave it mouldering here.'

'It does,' said Bill. 'Well – the only thing we can do is to carry it into a cool place somewhere and hope that boy will come back!'

They picked up the food and went into a nearby building. There was a hole in the floor, shaded by a half-ruined wall. They packed all the food there, wondering what would happen to it.

'Now we'd better go down to the creek and see if we can find the entrance, or whatever it is, shown on the map,' said Bill. He pulled it out of his pocket and looked at it. The children looked too. 'We shan't find it, so don't think it!' said Bill, who was secretly of the opinion that there was nothing to be discovered in this poor, 'dead' island.

They went down the overgrown, stone-strewn street and came to the rocky creek. The motor boat was there, rocking gently. Andros was fast asleep on the shady side of the boat.

The little party walked down the rocky ledge to the boat. Then they looked up the creek. Bill gave an exclamation. 'Of course! That's it!'

'*What*, Bill?' said the children at once.

'Well, "Two-Fingers" is marked on the map, apparently for no reason at all. The expert swore that's what the old Greek word meant. I just thought it might be an old name for someone – but now I see what it meant. Look up there.'

The children looked where Bill pointed, and above their heads some way away to the left they saw a peculiar rock. It was like a clenched hand with two fingers raised! Yes – two fingers. There they were. And 'Two-Fingers' was marked on the map!

'Come on. That's a guide of some sort,' said Bill, and they climbed along till they came to the queer two-fingered rock. They found a hole behind it, a hole that would quite easily allow a person to step into it. Bill fumbled for a torch. He switched it on.

'There may be a passage of some kind,' he said. 'Yes – there is! This is really extraordinary! I think, Jack, you'd better go back to the boat and get a lantern or two if you can find them. My torch isn't too good.'

Jack sped down to the boat. Andros was still asleep. Jack spotted two lanterns and brought them carefully up to the two-fingered rock, handing them at awkward places to Philip, who had come to meet him.

'Good,' said Bill. 'We'll light these. I'll take one and you can take the other, Jack. I'll save my torch.'

They lit the oil lanterns inside the hole. It wasn't big enough for a cave. It really was just a large hole behind the strange-looking rock – but at the back was what looked like an entry into the hill. Could it possibly be the entrance shown in the map?

'Do you think it is, Bill?' asked Lucy-Ann eagerly,

when the lanterns were lit, and Bill held one up to peer into the narrow rocky passage behind the hole.

'No. I can't believe it is,' said Bill. 'It must have been known for years by everyone in the city, when it was alive with people. It's just a coincidence, I expect.'

The children, of course, didn't think it was. They felt very thrilled indeed as they made their way along the dark little passage. It went for a hundred yards and then came out into a wide space. Bill held up his lantern. It shone on to rocky walls – but what was that at the back? The wall looked different there.

He took his lantern over to it. The beam shone on to large blocks of stone built like a great irregular door. 'I wonder why that was built here,' said Bill, surprised. He swung the lantern round to light up the rest of the cave. The walls were of smooth, shiny rock. There was not the smallest opening there at all. The only opening was the one they had come in by from the narrow passage.

He swung the light on to the built-in stones again. Then he put the lantern down.

'This was built to block up some other opening,' he said at last. The children's hearts sank. 'It is immensely strong, as you can see for yourselves – a door of great blocks of stone, a door that can't possibly be opened, or got through in any way.'

'Bill – do you think it's blocking up the entrance shown on the map?' asked Jack, dismayed.

'Well, yes – I do,' said Bill. 'It's been built many,

many years – it's old, as you can see. Why it was built, goodness knows! Anyway, there it is – and we're stopped right at the very outset! If this is the way shown on the map, the way that one must follow to get to wherever the treasure was hidden, it's impossible to follow it. Quite impossible!'

'Oh, Bill!' said Lucy-Ann almost in tears. 'It's too bad. Isn't there *any* way through?'

'Well – send Micky to see,' said Bill. 'If there's even a small hole Micky will find it. You know what monkeys are. Send him, Philip.'

'Go, Micky – go and hunt about,' said Philip. Micky looked at him enquiringly. He did not like this business of exploring dark passages, but he leapt off Philip's shoulder and obediently went off on an exploration of his own. Kiki watched him and then flew to a ledge at the top of the immense stone doorway.

'Send for the doctor,' she said in a hollow voice. 'Polly's got a cold. Send for the doctor.'

Micky bounded up to join her. He scurried about, putting his paw here and there, into crannies and crevices. But obviously there was nothing to find, for he soon came back and leapt on to Philip's shoulder, nestling closely into his neck.

'No go,' said Bill. He set the lantern down on the floor, meaning to put the map away. Just as he was folding it up Lucy-Ann gave an astonished cry.

'What's the matter?' said Jack, startled.

'Look – what's that over there – on the floor? Surely, it's – it's – a *torch battery*!'

Philip saw the thing she meant and went to pick it up. He brought it to the light of the lamp. 'Yes – that's just what it is – an old worn-out battery from a torch rather like Bill's. Bill – you haven't dropped a battery, have you?'

'Of course not,' said Bill. 'Yes, this is certainly an old battery – somebody must have thrown it down and put a new battery into his torch – whoever he may be! We are obviously not the only ones to know this place!'

Lucy-Ann shivered. She was sorry she had spotted that battery now. It made her feel uneasy. Who had been in this walled-up cave, and why?

'Let's go, Bill,' she said. 'We can't do any good here – it's all walled up. Let's go back to Andros. I don't like this.'

'Right. We'll go back,' said Bill. 'In any case, we ought to go now. We've been here ages, and we've got to get back to the ship tonight. Come along.'

They made their way out of the cave, down the narrow passage in the rocky hill and came to the hole. They climbed round the two-fingered rock and made their way to the creek.

And then they got a terrible shock. The motor boat was gone! They stared as if they could not believe their eyes.

'Where's the boat?' said Dinah feebly.

They looked up the creek and down. No sign of the boat at all. How very extraordinary! And then Jack gave a cry and pointed out to sea.

'Isn't that it? Look – right out there?'

They all strained their eyes, and Bill nodded his head grimly. 'Yes – that looks like it. What on earth made Andros go off without us? What an astounding thing to do!'

'He was fast asleep in the boat when I got the lantern,' said Jack. 'Never stirred. Everything seemed all right then.'

'Blessed if I understand it,' said Bill, looking bewildered. 'He seemed a good trustworthy chap – and I haven't even paid him. What in the world has possessed him to act like that?'

'That boat's going pretty fast,' said Philip. 'Almost out of sight now. Well, well, well – here we are marooned on our treasure island, sure as eggs are eggs!'

Lucy-Ann was very much alarmed. She took Bill's arm. 'What are we going to do?' she said. 'Are we to stay here, Bill?'

'Lucy-Ann, of course we are,' said Jack before Bill could answer. 'Where are we to go if we don't stay here? Have you got an aeroplane stowed away somewhere, ready for this emergency?'

'Shut up, Jack,' said Bill, putting his arm round Lucy-Ann. 'We shall be all right, don't fret, Lucy-Ann. It's only one of our adventures!'

19

All kinds of shocks

They stood there for a little while, not certain what to do. It was all so very unexpected. Then Bill shook himself and grinned round at the others.

'Well – it looks as if we've got to spend the night here, doesn't it? – and get our supper ourselves. Thank goodness we've got the food that extraordinary boy brought on his donkey! And Jack's got the rest of our picnic lunch as well.'

'Oh, *yes* – I'd forgotten that!' said Dinah, pleased. She had been thinking they would have nothing to eat.

'We can go and tuck in straight away,' said Bill. 'We'll find somewhere to sleep all right – it's very warm, and we shan't come to any harm. I don't particularly want to go and find one of those farms we saw, in case Andros takes it into his head to call back for us. He must have gone crazy.'

It was a curious evening that they all spent on Thamis. They went to find the store of food and had a very good meal indeed. They put the rest of it safely back in the cool place they had stored it in at first. Then they went wandering round the silent, ruined old city again. Lucy-Ann found an old pot with a broken neck, which she was very pleased with. Jack found some kind of metal fork – at least that is what he took it to be – with two of its prongs gone.

Bill had been hunting about for some place to sleep in. He had not been very successful. At last he chose a room not far from the ruined temple, one that had three walls and a little roof left. It was overgrown with thick grass but would have to do for a bedroom.

The sun was going down. It would soon be gone. Bill decided to put the food in the 'bedroom' too – it would be handy if they wanted any. He and the boys removed it from the place it was in and put it carefully in some thick, cool grass. They were glad there was such a lot!

When the sun disappeared everyone felt tired. Lucy-Ann was yawning her head off, and so was Kiki. Micky explored the ruined little room thoroughly, approved of it and settled down on Philip as soon as the boy had made himself a fairly soft bed in the thickly growing grass.

The four children fell asleep at once. Kiki perched herself quietly on Jack's middle as soon as she knew he was asleep. He had pushed her off two or three times, but this time he did not wake, and she remained where she was, her head tucked under her wing.

Bill lay and looked up at the stars he could see through the holes in the roof. He was angry with himself for bringing the children to Thamis. Now they had landed in difficulties again – all because of a legendary and most elusive treasure, one that certainly had not existed for years – if it had ever existed at all!

He puzzled over the boy on the donkey who had brought the food. He puzzled over the blocked-up entrance and the battery Lucy-Ann had found. But more than anything he puzzled over the sudden disappearance of Andros.

He was just about to fall off to sleep when he heard a noise. Micky must have heard it too, because he stirred and his small head looked round the 'bedroom'. Bill lay and listened, holding his breath. *Was* it a noise he had heard?

Then he heard the unmistakable sound of a voice! Then another voice, deep and complaining. Where did they come from?

He sat up cautiously and listened again. The voices came once more, and then Bill heard footsteps – footsteps coming down the ruined city street! He did not like it at all. Who on earth was walking through the old dead city in the middle of the night?

Kiki had heard the voices too. She flew out of the room she was in and hid herself under the ledge of an arch, waiting. The footsteps came nearer. The voices came too, talking together. Bill silently posted himself beside a broken window opening and watched. There was only starlight to see by, but he might be able to make out something.

Two dark figures came up the street. They stopped every now and again. It seemed to Bill as if they were looking in the ruined buildings to find something. Would they look into this one and find the children? Bill debated whether he should go out and accost these people. Who were they, anyway?

Then he decided that people who walk the streets of a ruined city at dead of night are not perhaps the best people to ask help from, and he remained where he was.

The two dark figures arrived nearby. He heard their voices again, but they spoke in a foreign language – Greek, probably – and he could not understand a word. They were obviously looking for something, Bill thought – and then he suddenly guessed what it was.

The food, perhaps! Maybe the boy had brought it for *them* – and they had not been there – but Bill had, and had got it instead. Now the men were looking for it, sure that the boy had dumped it somewhere.

'They'll look in here then, sure as anything,' thought Bill. But they didn't. Just as they got to the broken doorway, near where the parrot was perched, Kiki went off like a pistol shot.

CRACK!

The children all woke up at once and sat up. They

were too startled to make a sound, and as soon as they heard Bill's 'Shh!' they sat silently waiting.

The two men were most alarmed. Bill could see them clutching one another. They said something rapidly, obviously asking each other what that noise was.

Kiki considered them. She didn't like them. She began to cackle with laughter, and this horrified the men more than anything else could have done. Kiki's laughter was so completely idiotic that it froze them to the marrow.

Kiki stopped. She swelled out her throat and began to make her famous noise of an express train screeching through a tunnel, getting louder and louder and louder. It was a magnificent effort and had very satisfactory results.

The men yelled too, in panic, and set off as fast as they could, certain that something terrible was coming after them. Kiki sent another pistol shot after them and then relapsed into cackles.

'Well, really, Kiki,' said Bill, when the two men were completely gone. 'What a performance!'

'Who was it out there, Bill?' asked Dinah.

'I've no idea,' said Bill. 'But I have a feeling it was two hungry fellows come to look for the food the small boy presented us with today. Anyway, they've departed in a great hurry.'

'Kiki was marvellous, wasn't she?' said Jack. 'Good old Kiki! Clever bird!'

Kiki gave an outsize hiccup. 'Pardon! Send for the doctor! Pop goes the weasel.'

'Yes. Very nice. But that's enough now,' said Jack. 'Bill, who do you think those men were?'

'I've just told you – I've no idea,' said Bill. 'This place beats me. Come on, let's go to sleep again. I don't somehow think those fellows will come back – and if we have any other visitors I've no doubt Kiki will deal with them!'

They settled themselves off to sleep again. Bill lay awake wondering a little more, then he too fell asleep. He did not wake till morning.

The others were already awake. Jack had awakened very thirsty and had gone to look for water. He found a well beside a tumbledown house some way down the hill, and saw water in it. It was not long before he had rigged up a way of bringing up the water, which was crystal clear and cold. He tied string round the broken pot Lucy-Ann had found and lowered it down the well. It did not hold much water because the neck was broken, but it was enough for them all to quench their thirst. They had breakfast off the rolls and cheeses, and hoped the boy would come again that day!

'Go down and see if there's any sign of the boat, Jack,' said Bill when they had finished. So off he went, and soon came back to report that the creek was empty. No boat was anywhere to be seen.

'Well – we shall just have to wait about, that's all,'

said Bill. 'It will only be a question of time till we are taken off. Tim will wonder what's happened, for one thing. Or Andros will discover he's done a crazy thing, and come back for us!'

At about twelve o'clock they heard the dong-dong-dong of the donkey's bell again, and round the same corner came the imp of a boy. Bill knew what to do this time! He and the others unpacked the food, the boy was paid and, with the donkey's bell ringing loudly, he departed, much better pleased with his reception. Everyone stared after him.

'Really very extraordinary,' said Bill. 'Let's hide the food quickly, before the real recipients come along. We'll have a meal ourselves too. I'm hungry!'

They dragged the food to the room in which they had slept the night before, and had a good meal before they hid the rest. Bill wondered if he should find his way to one of the farms for help. But what help could they give? And what kind of a reception would he get? Anything might happen to him on this lonely island. He might be robbed and kept prisoner, or even killed.

Jack asked Bill to give him the map to study – the redrawn one. 'Not that it's going to be much use,' said Jack with a grin. 'Now that I'm on Thamis I don't think so much of it as I did. And it's difficult to believe in treasure when all you can see around you is a lot of ruins.'

Bill gave him the map. Jack took it into the space

once occupied by the temple, and sat down in a corner. Lucy-Ann came to sit with him. Kiki settled between them, murmuring companionably.

The two red heads bent over the map together. 'It's got so many things on it that I can't make anything out,' said Jack. '"Two-Fingers" – well, we know what that means, all right – and now look here – a lot further on it says "Bell". Well, what does that mean? Bell! What has a bell? A donkey, of course – and schools have bells – and—'

'Churches,' said Lucy-Ann. 'I expect this old temple had a bell once upon a time. I wonder where it was.'

She looked round and about but could see no place where a bell could have hung.

Jack looked at her suddenly. 'Lucy-Ann – of *course* – a temple *would* have a bell. The temple may be one of the clues, one of the guides to the treasure.'

'Do you think so?' said Lucy-Ann doubtfully. 'But – surely the treasure would have been hidden deep *underground* somewhere – not in the temple up here. We know the entrance to the secret passage was far *down* the hill, just above the creek.'

'Would it be hidden *under* the temple, perhaps?' said Jack. 'Or somewhere near? Maybe the temple had vaults. I say – that's an idea! If this one once had vaults, they must still be there. *Vaults* don't become ruins, like buildings. They're not exposed to wind and rain and sun. Vaults! Yes – going deep down into the hill – reached by an underground passage from the creek – a passage that could be approached easily enough from the sea – could be used by sailors who wanted to smuggle in goods. Lucy-Ann, there must be vaults! Come on – we'll look for them.'

Lucy-Ann, half excited, half disbelieving, got up and followed Jack. He began to hunt all over what must have once been the courtyard. It was too overgrown to tell if any way could be found underground.

They leaned against a great half-broken column to rest themselves. There was a large piece out of the column just above their heads, and Kiki flew up there to perch. At that moment Micky came bounding into the old courtyard of the temple, followed by the others. He saw Kiki and leapt up beside her.

She wasn't expecting him, and was startled and angry. She gave him such a violent nip that he lost his balance on the ledge – and fell backwards into the inside of the enormous column!

He shrieked with fright as he fell, and Kiki poked her head inside the hole to see what had happened to him.

'All gone,' she announced in a hollow voice. 'All gone. Ding-dong-bell.'

'You idiot, Kiki!' shouted Philip. 'Hey, Micky, Micky! Come on up!'

But there was no Micky. Only a little whimpering cry came up. 'He's hurt,' said Philip. 'Here, Jack, give me a leg-up. I'll go down into the column after him. He can't have fallen very far.'

Jack gave him a leg-up. He got on to the broken place, swung his legs in and was about to jump down when he stopped and looked in cautiously.

'Hey, Bill!' he called. 'Hand me your torch. I'd better look before I leap, I think. There's something odd here!'

Bill handed him up his torch. Philip switched it on and looked down into the hollow of the great column. He turned and looked back at the others.

'I say – it's amazing. It looks as if there's steps at the bottom of this column! What do you think of *that*?'

20

Exploring the treasure route

Everyone was amazed. Steps! Stone steps leading down-ward at the base of the hollow stone column! Jack gave a loud whoop.

'I bet they go to the vaults!'

'*What* vaults?' asked Dinah in astonishment. But Jack was too excited to tell her.

'Bill – let's go down. Come on. We're on the track of the treasure. Didn't the map say "Bell"? Well, the temple must have a bell. I bet the treasure's somewhere under-neath!'

'You're talking double Dutch,' said Bill, not following this at all. 'Philip – come down. Don't attempt any scatterbrained exploration till we get the lanterns, and till I have a look myself. Do you hear me?'

'Yes, right, Bill,' said Philip reluctantly, and jumped down. 'Micky's down there somewhere – he must have fallen on the steps and gone bumping down. I can still hear him whimpering.'

'I expect he got a bit of a shock,' said Bill. 'Go and get the lanterns and also the food, you boys. If we are going underground, we'd better prepare ourselves!'

Before the boys returned Micky had come back – a Micky very frightened and sorry for himself indeed. He looked for his beloved Philip but he wasn't there, so he went to Lucy-Ann and let her nurse him like a baby. He whimpered all the time, and Lucy-Ann was very distressed.

'Now, now – you haven't really hurt yourself,' she consoled him. 'Just a bruise or two, I expect. It was very, very naughty of Kiki. Still, you've made a wonderful find, Micky. Really wonderful!'

Kiki was very ashamed of herself. She went into a corner and put her head under her wing. Nobody took any notice of her at all.

The boys came back. Bill had had a good look down the hollow column with his torch. It puzzled him how the ancient folk, who had used the column as a way of getting underground, had made an entry in it. He could see no way of entry at all – except, of course, through the great hole broken in the column.

'It's a narrow spiral stairway,' he told the girls. 'Probably Jack is right. It may lead down to the vaults of the temple – a very secret way to them, possibly known only to the head priest. Come on, boys – help the girls up. I'll go down first.'

He dropped down deftly to the head of the steps. He

shone his torch down. Yes, it was a spiral stairway, as he had thought. It would be very narrow here, but probably got wider lower down. He had almost to crawl down the first twelve steps, and two or three times he nearly slipped because the treads were so narrow and steep.

The girls followed, helped by the boys. Dinah took one lantern, finding it very difficult indeed to manage with it, and at last had to hand it down to Bill because she needed both her hands at the top of the stairway. Lucy-Ann went down by the light of the second lantern, held by Jack.

The food was dropped in behind them. 'Might as well leave it there,' called back Bill. 'We can fetch it if we need it – and it's as good a hiding place as anywhere else.'

So they left the food at the top of the stairway on a stone ledge, and pretty soon all five were a good way down. As Bill had thought, the stone steps grew very much wider and easier a little further on.

Micky was now on Philip's shoulder again. Kiki had followed Jack into the column, very quiet and subdued. Down they went and down.

They came to the end of the stairway. It finished in a vast cave or vault that stretched out endlessly in the rock of the hill. The lanterns only lit up a small part of it.

'Yes – here are the vaults all right,' said Jack. 'The way we've come to them must have been a very secret one, I should think. Look – there's another way up, Bill – over there – more stone steps – straight ones this time, not spiral – going quite steeply upward.'

'Yes. I should think that was the ordinary way used up and down to the vaults,' said Bill. 'The way we came is very well hidden. See, from here you can't even see it, hidden behind that enormous rock.'

He swung his torch up the wide sweep of steps to which they had now walked over. 'I'll go up and see where they lead to,' said Bill, and up he went. They heard his steps going up and up, and then they stopped. They heard them coming down again.

'Came up against a stone ceiling!' he reported. 'Probably there's an exit there, closed up by a great stone trapdoor overgrown now with weeds and grass. That was obviously the ordinary way in and out. Well, where do we go from here?'

'Bill, let's look at the map again,' said Jack. 'I'm sure we must now be at the place marked "Bell". "Bell" for temple, you know.'

By the light of Bill's torch they all pored over the map again. Bill traced the 'Treasure path' with his finger. '"Two-Finger Rock",' he said. 'We were there, and were stopped by the walled-in place.'

'Yes – then the next thing marked is "Goddess",' said Philip. 'Can't think what *that* means!'

'Something on the way from "Two-Finger Rock" to here, perhaps,' said Jack. 'We could go and see. Then look – there comes "Tomb". I suppose that's where someone was buried.'

'Yes – in a stone cell, I should think,' said Bill. 'And then we come to "Bird", which seems rather strange.'

'Then to "Bell",' said Jack triumphantly. 'And that's where *we* are, I bet!'

'Yes – but not where the treasure is,' said Bill. 'Look – you go on to here – marked "Labyrinth". Not so good, that.'

'What's a labyrinth, exactly?' asked Lucy-Ann.

'A maze – a place where it's so winding and muddling that you can easily get lost,' said Dinah. Lucy-Ann did not like the sound of that at all!

'Labyrinth,' she said. 'Well, what's next?'

'"Catacomb",' said Bill. 'And that, apparently, is where the treasure was put! What a way to bring it!'

'Let's go and find it!' said Jack cheerfully. He folded up the map and put it into his pocket. 'Come on – we've got nothing else to do. I must say it's nice and cool down here after the heat up above in the sun!'

'The thing is – which way do we go?' said Bill. 'One way goes to the "Labyrinth," the other to the "Tomb". But although the points of the compass are marked on the map to make things easy, we're not able to see the sun, so we have no idea of direction. Anyone got a compass?'

Nobody had. 'Well – we'll have to guess,' said Bill.

'There's only two ways to go apparently – to the right or to the left. Let's go right.'

So they set off to the right of the vault – Bill with his torch, the two girls holding hands and each boy carrying a lantern. The shadows were weird, and the hollow echo of their feet strange and rather alarming. Kiki and Micky did not like it at all, and they sat silent on the boys' shoulders.

They went for some way and then came to a wide passage that led downward in a smooth slope. It went for a good way, and then stopped short at what appeared to be a door. It was a wooden door and had once been immensely stout and strong. Even now it was still good, but one of the hinges had given way and, as the children first pushed and then pulled it, the other hinges gave way too and the door fell inward, almost on top of Bill. He just leapt away in time.

He shone his torch on it. Carved right across the door was an enormous bird. 'There you are – "Bird",' said Jack, pleased. 'That was one of the clues, wasn't it, Bill? It's an eagle – beautifully carved too.'

'Now we know which way we're going – the wrong way!' said Bill. 'Still, we'll go on now – this is amazing!'

Leaving the fallen Bird-door behind, they went through the opening. Looking back, they saw that the passage they were now following forked into two by the door – evidently there were two ways to go there – and the right one was the Bird-door – hence the clue called "Bird".

They went down a very narrow passage indeed. It ran downward, as the other had done, until it opened out into a narrow chamber. There was a smooth stone ledge at one side. At each end were wooden slabs carved with intricate symbols. The little company stopped to look at them.

'This must have been a tomb,' said Bill. 'Possibly where a priest was buried. There are many old burial places like this.'

'The sailors who carried the treasure must have had to carry it through this tomb,' said Philip. 'Perhaps they knew this way because they robbed tombs.'

There was no door to the tomb, but the doorway was cut out smooth and level. Possibly there had once been a door. Beyond it the passage began again, sloping downward more steeply still.

'Now for "Goddess",' said Jack. 'I say – it's a pretty good guide, this map, isn't it, Bill? If we had been able to make our way through "Two-Finger Rock" – where the hole was, you know – we could have used the map as an absolutely accurate guide.'

'Look out – there are steps,' said Bill. 'Cut into the rock. It gets pretty steep here.'

They went carefully down the steps. At the bottom was a beautiful archway. It was made of some kind of marble, set into the natural archway of the rock. Beyond the arch was a marble floor, still smooth and shining, for there was no dust underground.

The walls were carved too, the solid rock itself chipped out into figures and symbols. Eagles, doves, foxes, wolves – curious designs and patterns decorated the whole of the strange little cave.

'This must be "Goddess",' said Bill. 'A place to worship some little-known goddess, I imagine – hidden under the ground, only to be visited in secret.'

'Yes – that must be it,' said Philip. 'Isn't it strange? I suppose those carvings are hundreds of years old!'

'And now for the last clue – or first, whichever you like to call it,' said Bill. '"Two-Fingers"! We know what that is, anyway. But we shall come up against the other side of the stone door, I've no doubt. Here we go. My word, it's steep now, isn't it? No steps either. Be careful, you girls!'

They made their way, stumbling, down a very steep passage – and, just as Bill had said, they came up against the other side of the walled-up doorway they had seen when they had gone into 'Two-Fingers' hole. They stopped and considered.

'Yes – we've found the treasure route all right,' said Bill. 'Now – we'll start from here again – "Two-Fingers" – and we'll work our way back – past "Goddess" and "Tomb" and "Bird", till we come to "Bell" – the temple vault.'

'And *then* we'll go on!' said Jack, almost trembling with excitement. 'On to "Labyrinth" and "Catacomb" – and "TREASURE"!'

21

Kiki is very tiresome

Back they all went, through the curious little cell that must once have been a marble temple underground dedicated to some strange goddess – through the old tomb, and over the fallen door carved with the bird – and soon they were back in the temple vault.

'Now we start off the other way – to the left,' said Bill, who was now almost as excited as the four children. 'Come along – down this passage here. Hold up your lantern, Philip. My torch isn't very strong.'

'Does this passage lead into the labyrinth – the maze where people get lost?' asked Lucy-Ann a little fearfully. 'Shall *we* get lost?'

'No. We'll find some way of keeping safe,' said Bill. He and Jack looked closely at the map. 'Although this part is marked "Labyrinth", it shows only one route or passage – but every now and again the letter "R" turns up – for "Right", I suppose. We seem to have to turn to the right six times. Well, if we come to a fork, we shall know what to do – right every time! Come along! Put the map back in your pocket, Jack.'

They went down the low-roofed winding passage for a little way, and then Jack called out to the others. 'I say – anyone got Kiki?'

They all stopped. 'I haven't,' yelled back Lucy-Ann. 'Nor has Dinah.' Bill said he certainly hadn't, and as for Philip, he only had Micky on his shoulder.

'She flew off my shoulder when we got into the vault,' said Jack, remembering. 'Kiki! KIKI! Where are you?'

There was no squawk or screech in reply. 'Blow!' said Jack. 'I'll have to go back and get her. I'll catch you up.'

He ran back. The others went on. Jack had a lantern and could easily catch them up.

They soon came to a fork. 'We take the right-hand one,' said Bill. 'This way!' The passage twisted and turned extraordinarily often, and it was impossible to know if they were going forward, or if by so much turning and twisting were going in the opposite direction.

'One right turn – two – and this is the third,' said Philip. 'Three more right turns and we'll be at the catacomb!'

'Ooooh,' said Lucy-Ann. 'I hope it won't be long! I'm tired of these dark passages. This one is stony – I keep hitting my toes against some stone or other.'

'I wish Jack would catch us up,' said Philip, who was last. 'I keep thinking I hear him behind me – and when I turn he isn't there. Ought we to wait for him, Bill?'

'Yes – perhaps we ought,' said Bill, and they stopped. But no Jack came. Gracious, what *could* he be doing? Lucy-Ann began to feel worried.

'Jack!' she called. 'JACK! Are you coming?'

'Better go back for him,' said Bill, puzzled. 'I hope to goodness he hasn't missed the way. He knew we had to turn right each time.'

They went back for some way – and then Bill stopped. 'I suppose *we're* right?' he said. 'I don't somehow remember this passage – it's got such a very, very low roof. I've just bumped my head against it, and I certainly didn't do that coming along!'

'Oh, dear – surely we haven't missed our way – it seemed so easy – turn to the left each time going back,' groaned Dinah. 'It *must* be right, Bill.'

Bill was uneasy. He certainly did not remember this low-roofed passage. He made up his mind. 'We'll go back,' he said. 'I think we missed the last left turn, somehow.'

So they went back – but soon they came to a dead stop! The passage grew narrower and narrower, and at last nobody could squeeze through. *That* couldn't be right, either!

'Wrong again,' said Bill much more cheerfully than he felt. Secretly he was scared and horrified. How big was this labyrinth? How far did it go into the hill? On the map it looked a short route – but the labyrinth itself might spread for miles, intersected by mazes of passages, criss-crossing, wandering round and round.

'It's a real maze,' thought Bill. 'And probably there are only one or two direct routes across it – and we've missed the one we ought to have taken. Goodness knows how long we'll be wandering about here!'

'I wonder where Jack is,' said Lucy-Ann anxiously as they wound in and out of the curious passages of the labyrinth. 'I do hope he's all right.'

Where *was* Jack? He had gone back to get Kiki, and had heard her talking mournfully to herself in the temple vault, perched on the spiral stone stairway that led up to the broken column. He called her.

'Kiki! What are you doing there? Why didn't you come with us, idiot? Now I've had to come all the way back for you!'

Kiki was tired of being underground. She wanted to go up into the sunshine. Also she wanted a drink and there seemed to be no water below the ground.

'Kiki! Come along! I want to get back to the others,' called Jack.

'Send for the doctor,' said Kiki, preening her wings. 'Polly's got a cold, send for the doctor.'

'Don't be so *tiresome*,' said Jack, exasperated, and he went over to where Kiki sat. She flew up a few steps and cocked her head at Jack. He could see her plainly in the light of his lantern, and he was cross.

'You're behaving very badly,' he scolded her. 'Come down and sit on my shoulder, bad bird.'

'Naughty Polly, send for the doctor,' said Kiki, who seemed to have got the doctor on her brain. She flew up a few more steps. Jack had to follow. Blow Kiki! She *would* behave like this just when he wanted to catch up the others.

He reached the parrot and she flew higher again. Finally she disappeared.

Jack yelled up the stone steps angrily. 'You wait till I get you, you bad bird! Playing me up like this! For the last time, come down!'

A mocking voice floated down to him. 'Wipe your feet, don't sniff, pop goes the doctor!'

That was really too much for poor Jack! He climbed the spiral stone stairs as fast as he could, finding it very difficult indeed at the top, where they came up at the bottom of the broken column. At last he stood inside the column. He could see very well now, for the sun shone in through the hole in the stone. Kiki was sitting on the broken edge of the hole, preening herself in the sun. She kept a lookout for Jack, knowing he was very cross.

'Oh, I say!' she said loudly. 'Oh, I say!' She flew off the edge of the hole and disappeared from Jack's view. He could still hear her calling out, though. 'Oh, I say! Oh, I say!'

Saying all kinds of rude things about Kiki under his

breath, Jack found a rough foothold in the inside of the column and heaved himself up to the hole. He swung himself through the hole and jumped down into the sunshine, looking round for Kiki.

There she sat, not far off, in a tree of some kind, peering down the hill. 'Oh, I say!' she cried in a shrill voice, and then went off into a cackle of laughter.

Jack ran to the tree angrily – and then he stopped. Someone was coming up the hill – someone quite familiar – astonishingly familiar! Someone with teeth that stuck out in front, and with a chin that was hardly there at all!

'*Lucian!*' said Jack, too astonished to move. And Lucian it was. No wonder Kiki had suddenly gone off into a stream of 'Oh, I says!' Lucian stopped and stared at Jack as if he really could not believe his eyes.

'Oh, I say!' he said. 'Oh, I SAY.'

'Hello,' said Jack feebly, and grinned. 'Er – what in the world are *you* doing here?'

'Well, I might say the same to you,' said Lucian. 'Of all the extraordinary things! Well, I never! I can't believe it!'

'How long have you been here?' asked Jack. 'Why are you here?'

'I only came today,' said Lucian. 'My uncle's here, you see – goodness knows why! I don't know when he came exactly. Anyway, he got here and then sent for another motor boat to come to him here on Thamis, bringing some men he wanted, and some goods – and I thought I'd come along too. The *Viking Star* is held up, as you know, and I was bored stiff. I suppose my uncle's going to get some antiques here or something.'

Jack digested all this in silence. Oho! So Mr Eppy was there too, was he? He was hot on the track after all. Jack thought quickly. What a pity he had met Lucian! Now the boy would tell Mr Eppy.

'Jack, what are *you* doing here? You really must tell me!' said Lucian insistently. 'It's *too* extraordinary. And Kiki too! Where are the others?'

'Why should they be here?' said Jack. He did not want to tell Lucian about them – or where they were – or how to get to them. That would never do. He thought hard, but he could not come up with a plan – except that if he could get rid of Lucian he would pop down the broken column, get down the spiral stairway to the vault, and warn Bill. Bill would know what to do.

How could he get rid of Lucian? Lucian wasn't likely to let him out of his sight at all. And blow, blow, blow! – there was Mr Eppy coming up the hillside now with three other men!

Mr Eppy was too surprised to speak when he suddenly caught sight of Jack and Kiki. He stopped dead and stared through his dark glasses. He took them off, rubbed them, and was about to put them on again when Lucian went off into one of his silly fits of giggling.

'Oh dear! Oh, I say! You can't believe your eyes, can you, Uncle? Nor could I. But it really *is* Jack – and Kiki the parrot too.'

For one wild moment Jack wondered if he should run for it – run from the surprised men and hide somewhere till he could manage to get back to Bill and warn him.

But there was no time. At a word from Mr Eppy the three men with him ran up and stationed themselves behind Jack. Then Mr Eppy came up and stood in front of him.

'And what exactly are *you* doing here?' he said, in such a peculiar, menacing tone that Jack was astonished and scared. 'Where are the others?'

'We came to explore a bit,' said Jack at last. 'That's all. Anyone can come and explore these islands. The *Viking Star*'s engines broke down and the passengers were told they could hire motor boats and cruise among these islands.'

'Why did you come to *this* one?' asked Mr Eppy, still in a fierce voice. Lucian answered unexpectedly for him.

'Oh, Uncle! I expect he came hunting for the treasure you told me about.'

'Hold your tongue, idiot of a boy,' said Mr Eppy, almost spitting at poor Lucian. 'And now *you*' – he turned to Jack again – 'how dare you come trespassing on *my* island!'

'It isn't yours,' said Jack.

'It is. I have just bought it!' said Mr Eppy. 'Ah – you didn't know that – but you know *why*!'

22

Mr Eppy again

Yes, Jack did know why Mr Eppy had bought the island. He stared at the man miserably, his heart sinking. If the island was Mr Eppy's, then the treasure would be his too. Once again it looked as if the adventure had come to a sudden end.

'You know *why* I have bought it?' repeated Mr Eppy. 'Tell me, boy.'

'Well – I suppose you wanted to look for treasure on it,' said Jack in a low tone. 'But you won't find it. You only saw two pieces of the map, remember!'

'Then you will tell me what was on the other pieces,' said Mr Eppy in a dangerous tone.

Lucian was by now looking distinctly frightened. 'Here, I say, Uncle,' he began. 'I don't think you ought to talk to old Jack like that, you know. I mean to say . . .'

Mr Eppy took a step backwards and slapped Lucian neatly across the mouth. His hand made a noise like a whip-crack and Kiki immediately imitated it. Then she scolded Mr Eppy. 'Naughty boy, naughty boy, nit-wit, mister-sir!'

Lucian burst into howls. He put his hand up to his mouth, and stumbled away to a corner. The three men did not turn a hair.

'That is how I treat foolish boys,' said Mr Eppy, turning back to Jack. 'Are you going to be foolish too?'

Jack said nothing. Mr Eppy put his face close to his, and hissed at him so startlingly that Jack took a sudden step back and trod on the foot of one of the three men.

'Where are the others?' demanded Mr Eppy with his face close to Jack's. 'They must be here too. I sent away your boat yesterday. I threatened the man with prison for daring to land people on my island!'

'Oh – so *that's* why Andros ran away,' said Jack in disgust. 'What a foolish thing to do, Mr Eppy! Don't you know he'll come back again, probably with help?'

'He won't,' said Mr Eppy. 'He knows I shall put him in prison if he opens his mouth. No, no – I knew what I was doing. When I saw the boat there I guessed you and that big friend of yours were interfering here. I have heard of him! This is *my* island! Everything on it is mine.'

'All right, all right,' said Jack. 'But why send the boat away without us? Why not send us off too? If you had told us it was yours – and I know you do buy and sell islands – we wouldn't have trespassed without permission.'

'I wanted you here,' said Mr Eppy. 'You have the

plan, have you not? You did not leave it behind you? Ah, no – you would bring such a precious thing with you!'

Jack was silent. Of course – that was why Mr Eppy had sent the boat away without them – he meant to get the plan! And as he thought of that, Jack also thought of something else – something absolutely maddening.

He had the plan on him – the re-drawn one. He had looked at it with Bill underground, and had not given it back! Suppose Mr Eppy searched him. He would most certainly find it. How could he destroy it before he was searched?

'It was you, I suppose, who met the farmboy yester-day, and today too, and took the food I had sent for,' said Mr Eppy. 'A most extraordinary thing to do! I am not pleased with things like that – they make trouble for me.'

'Well – goodness gracious – how in the world were we to know that the food was for *you*, when we didn't know you were here, and couldn't understand a word the boy said?' cried Jack. 'Your boat wasn't in the creek. We didn't know anyone else was visiting the island.'

'I came to the other creek,' said Mr Eppy. 'But I shall not tell you where it is. No – not till you tell me where the others are – and then, when I have the plan, maybe, I say *maybe*, I will set you free from this island – all of you who have come to interfere with my plans.'

'It's ridiculous,' said Jack in disgust. 'We haven't come to interfere. Bill would be the first to say we'd all go, if he knew you had bought the island.'

'Where are the others?' barked Mr Eppy suddenly.

'Somewhere about,' said Jack indifferently. 'Why don't you look for them? And don't shout at me like that. I'm not Lucian.'

'Has this Bill the plan?' asked Mr Eppy, his voice getting sharper.

'Why don't you find him and ask him?' said Jack. 'Call him! See if he answers! If I'm here why shouldn't he be?'

Mr Eppy gave Jack such a sudden box on the ears that the boy had no time to dodge it. Kiki almost got the slap too, but rose into the air in time. She pounced down on the angry man and gave his ear such a vicious nip that he yelled in agony.

Jack suppressed a smile. Serve him right! Good old Kiki! The parrot sailed to a high branch and perched there, scolding hard.

'Bad boy, naughty boy! Gr-r-r-r! Go to bed, go to the doctor, go to the weasel!'

Mr Eppy said something sharply to the three silent men behind Jack. In a trice they had him pinned by the arms, flat on the ground. Then, with a practised hand, one of the men searched him. He drew out the plan at once.

Mr Eppy took it. Jack could imagine how his eyes gleamed behind the dark glasses!

'And so! *You* had it,' said Mr Eppy. He unfolded it, and saw that it was not the original plan. He looked at it closely. 'What is this? It is drawn by someone who has seen the other one – it's been drawn for you. Has it been deciphered and translated?'

'Find out for yourself,' said Jack, still lying on the ground. He expected a kick or a blow, but Mr Eppy was so intent on the re-drawn plan that he did nothing. Jack remembered that the man had seen only two parts of the map before – enough to tell him which island to come to, and that there was treasure there. He must now be studying the other parts with eager interest.

'"Two-Fingers",' he muttered. Then he looked at Jack. '"Two-Fingers",' he said. 'That showed on the piece I saw before – and I found the two-fingered rock. But there is no way through.'

'Oh – so that was your old battery we found in the hole, I suppose,' said Jack, sitting up. 'We wondered whose it was.'

Mr Eppy did not answer, or seem even to hear him. He was studying the map again. He was muttering something to himself. '"Two-Fingers" – "Goddess" – "Tomb" – "Bird" – "Bell" – "Labyrinth" – "Catacomb" – that is the route they took. The whole of it!' Then he began to mutter in Greek, and Jack could no longer understand him.

Lucian was still holding his hand up to his mouth, and his face was tear-stained. Kiki was down by him, pecking at his shoelace. 'Oh, I say!' she was repeating. 'Oh, I say!'

'Have you found the way at all?' demanded Mr Eppy.

'What way?' said Jack innocently.

'Pah! The way to the treasure chamber!' spat Mr Eppy.

'Pah!' spat Kiki at once. 'Pah!'

'I'll wring that bird's neck,' threatened Mr Eppy. 'Answer my question, boy.'

'No, we haven't found the way,' said Jack truthfully, feeling quite glad that they had gone the wrong way and not the right one in their following of the route! All the same, he wondered if Bill and the others had managed to find the way by now without him. But surely they would have waited for him. They must be wondering what in the wide world had happened to him! Jack hoped fervently that they would not all come climbing out of the broken column. If they did they would be taken prisoner by Mr Eppy and his men, and Bill would find it extremely difficult to keep his secret. In fact, it would not be any good his trying, now Mr Eppy had the map.

'Once Mr Eppy knows the way down the broken column the treasure is as good as his!' thought Jack. 'What a good thing Lucian didn't spot me getting out of it! I only hope the others don't make a sudden appearance. I'm sure they will soon!'

But they did not, for the very simple reason that they had lost their way in the labyrinth! They were still wandering about the passages, getting more and more anxious. They had lost Jack, and had lost their way too.

'This awful maze!' said Dinah in despair. 'Look, Bill – I'm *sure* we've been in *this* passage before. I remember the way this horrid piece juts out – it knocked my elbow last time, and this time too. I'm sure it's the same.'

'We're going round and round and in and out, and goodness knows whether we're near the vault or near the catacomb!' groaned Philip.

Bill was very worried. He stood and thought for a moment, trying in vain to get a sense of direction. It was so difficult underground! He set off again, and soon came to a fork.

'Well,' he said, 'I vote we go right here. It may be one of the places where we're supposed to go right. So we'll hope for the best! Come on!'

They trailed after him, Lucy-Ann getting very weary of it all. They reached another fork and turned right once more. Then they came to where the passages branched into four. Again they took the right-hand fork. Bill was feeling a little more cheerful. Perhaps they were on the right road now. They no longer came to blind ends where they had to turn back as they had been doing before. Ah – here was another fork. Well, to the right again!

The passage ended abruptly in a downward flight of steep steps. Bill swung the lantern up high and peered down the steps.

'We've come the right way at last!' he said. 'These must be the catacombs – underground caves and passages all joined together, that were once used as hiding places, burial places and goodness knows what!'

'Oh, Bill – have we really come right?' said Lucy-Ann joyfully. 'I thought we were lost for ever and ever! Do we go down the steps?'

'We do,' said Bill. 'I'll go first. Come on.'

Down he went and the others followed carefully. There were about thirty steps, and it seemed to the children as if they really were going down into the bowels of the earth. At the end was a strange place stretching out into the darkness. Lining its walls were stone shelves, rocky niches, hollowed-out places that looked as if they had been used for storing things in, or for people to hide in and sleep.

They came to a hole in the floor of this extraordinary place. Bill shone his torch down it. It was a shaft leading downward, and there were footholds in the rock. 'I'm going down,' said Bill. 'I've got a hunch this is the place!'

He disappeared down the shaft with his torch, and soon his voice came back, excited and loud.

'This is it! This is the treasure chamber – THE TREASURE'S STILL HERE!'

23

Treasure – and trickery!

The three children and Micky almost fell down the shaft, they were in such a hurry. They handed Bill the lantern and, by the light of that and of Bill's torch, they looked in wonder round the curious treasure chamber.

It was perfectly round, as if it had been hollowed by machinery from the rock – though actually, of course, it had been done by hand. Thrown higgledy-piggledy into this enormous round cave – perhaps flung down the shaft in a hurry – were mouldering barrels and boxes and brass-bound chests.

Bursting out of them was a perfect medley of strange and amazing goods – chains of some kind of metal, set with precious stones – brooches, armlets, anklets – combs for the hair made probably of gold, and set with tiny stones – beautiful vases of metal, perhaps gold, perhaps brass, but too tarnished to tell. Beautifully wrought daggers lay in one corner, and what looked like armour of some kind in another – all fallen from the mouldered chests and boxes, or possibly burst out of these when they were thrown down the shaft so long, long ago.

There were broken models of figures and articles that looked like drinking cups and bowls, and yet other things whose use the children simply could not guess.

'Well, well, well,' said Bill, as thrilled as the children. 'What a treasure hoard! Andra's treasure, maybe – we shall never really know. But whether it is or not, it is certainly worth half a small kingdom because of its age! Look at this dagger – it must be hundreds of years old – perfectly preserved down in this dry shaft. I should think only our museums can show things like this now.'

'Bill! It's super!' said Philip, his eyes shining in the lantern-light as he picked up treasure after treasure, everything beautifully modelled and carved.

'I suppose the things like robes and cloaks and shoes have all mouldered away,' said Dinah regretfully. 'I'd like to have dressed up in those. Oh, Bill – we've really found it!'

'I wish Jack was here,' said Lucy-Ann, with tears in her voice. 'He would have loved it so. Where *can* he be, Bill?'

'I should think he probably took a long time finding Kiki and decided he wouldn't risk coming after us by himself,' said Bill. 'I'll tell you what we'll do – we'll go back and find him, and then we'll bring him here to have a look at the greatest treasure in the world!'

'But shall we be able to find our way back?' said Philip doubtfully. Bill was very doubtful about this too. Also his torch was giving out and he was sure the oil in the lantern would not last much longer. It was very necessary to find their way back, pick up Jack, and also have something to eat! Excitement had kept them going, but now all of them were feeling very hungry indeed.

'If we manage to get back quickly and find Jack we'll all have a meal,' said Bill. 'Then if Jack's lantern is all right we'll use that to come here again – but this time we'll be sensible and mark the walls as we go along! Actually I think we could find our way here easily enough if we concentrated on going right, right, right all the time. We must have missed one of the right turns.'

They climbed back up the shaft, leaving the extraordinary hiding place behind them. What a strange treasure chamber! How old was it? Had anyone else seen it since it had been put there?

They found themselves in the catacombs again. It was easy to get back to the steep flight of steps. Up they went into the labyrinth and began to make their way through the passages. 'Now we must keep left, left, left,' said Bill, 'then we shall be quite all right.'

But no – once more they missed their way and began the everlasting wandering round and round and in and out of the maddening underground maze. Lucy-Ann was almost crying with weariness.

All this time Micky had been quietly on Philip's shoulder, clinging to his head in awkward places. He too was tired of the curious dark walk that everyone was taking. He wanted to be out in the open, he wanted something to eat and, even more, he wanted something to drink.

He suddenly leapt off Philip's shoulder and landed on the floor of the passage. He began to scud along by himself. Philip called out to him.

'Hey, Micky, Micky! Come here! We don't want to lose you too!'

Micky slowed down, but he still went on. Bill called to Philip. 'Leave him, Philip! I believe he knows the way out. Animals have a good sense of direction, you know – a kind of homing instinct. Maybe he can take us straight to the broken column!'

Micky did not know what Bill was saying, but if he had known he would most certainly have agreed. Of course he knew the way! Of course his instinct told him exactly the right way to go – left, left, left, without any silly mistake such as the humans had made. Why, he, Micky, could have taken them straight back to the vaults at any time if only they had told him they wanted to go!

'Well, here we are in the vault again!' said Philip thankfully when, in a very short space of time indeed, they came out into the enormous temple vault. Lucy-Ann was so thankful that she began to cry very quietly to herself. Nobody could see. She wiped away a few tears, then stopped her crying, feeling rather ashamed. She slipped her hand into Bill's. He squeezed it comfortingly.

'We're all right now,' he said. 'We've found the treasure and found our way back – now we'll find Jack! As we haven't heard or seen anything of him, I imagine he's out in the open, waiting for us!'

Jack was still in the courtyard with Mr Eppy, Lucian and the three men. It was some time later, and the boy had not been having at all a nice time. Mr Eppy had been on and on at him, trying to find out where the others were, and whether Jack knew the route to the treasure.

He had threatened Jack, had boxed his ears several times, and had boxed Lucian's too when he had tried to come to Jack's help. Jack had been surprised at Lucian for that. He had always thought him such a feeble boy. He looked at Lucian gratefully.

'Thanks, Lucian,' he said. 'But don't interfere, old chap – you'll only get hurt. I can look after myself. Your uncle will get into trouble for ill-treating me, don't you worry!'

Jack had begun to feel extremely hungry. So had the others, presumably, because Mr Eppy changed the subject suddenly and began asking Jack where they had put the food they had got from the farm-boy. Jack remembered perfectly well where it was – inside the broken column, on the stone ledge at the base of it, where the stone stairway began – but how could he say that? It would give the secret away completely!

So he sat silent, shaking his head to Mr Eppy's exasperated questions, getting more and more hungry – and getting really rather anxious about the others too. Where in the world could they be? The sun was going down already, and soon it would be night.

And then Kiki began to talk excitedly. She left Jack and flew to the broken edge of the hole in the column. She peered down it. Jack bit his lip. Oh, Kiki, Kiki, don't give the game away!

Kiki had heard the others coming. She had heard Bill's deep voice as he came up the spiral stairway; she had heard Lucy-Ann's high voice just behind. She had gone to welcome them.

'Kiki!' called Jack. 'Come here.'

'Shut the door, shut the door, wipe your feet, beg your pardon!' shouted Kiki excitedly, her head inside the column. And then an answering call came from inside too.

'Hallo, Kiki, old bird! So there you are! Where's Jack?' It was Bill's cheery deep voice.

Mr Eppy sprang to attention at once. He gave a short sharp order to his three men, and they ran to the column to wait. Jack gave a yell.

'Look out, Bill! Danger! Look out!'

There was silence from inside the column. Then Bill's voice came up again.

'What's up?'

'Mr Epp . . .' began Jack, and was silenced as Mr Eppy placed a heavy and very rough hand over his mouth.

Bill shouted again. 'What's up?' As he got no reply he appeared at the hole in the column and swung himself astride the edge. The men were at the other side, hidden, waiting to spring.

Bill saw Mr Eppy apparently holding down Jack, and he leapt off the broken edge of the hole in the column at once. The three men sprang on him and bore him to the ground.

One sat on his head so that he could not shout. Jack squirmed under Mr Eppy's hand, kicking and trying to bite, but the man was very strong indeed.

Then up the column came Philip, wondering what had happened to Bill, and when he saw him being well and truly sat on he sprang to his rescue. Mr Eppy shouted a few words and the men released Bill. He sat up at once, feeling his nose, and wondering if any of his teeth were loose!

'What on earth is all this?' he began. But before he could go on, a call from inside the column came to him. It was Lucy-Ann.

'Bill! Oh, Bill! What's happened? Can we come out?'

Bill considered. 'I'm going to help the girls out,' he said to Mr Eppy, who nodded, and very soon both girls, and a very scared Micky, were standing in the old court-yard with Philip, Jack and Bill.

'What's happened?' said Lucy-Ann. 'Oh, I'm so glad to see you, Jack. I was dreadfully worried about you. Gracious, there's *Lucian*!'

'Oh, I say!' said Lucian, trying to put a brave face on things. 'Fancy meeting *you* here!'

Mr Eppy said something snappish in Greek and poor Lucian collapsed again. Then Mr Eppy turned to Bill, who was now eyeing him with a very sinister look indeed. Bill was extremely angry, and his injured nose was swelling rapidly.

'Look here, Eppy, or whatever your name is,' he said, 'you're going to run into serious trouble. You can't roam round with a posse of shady fellows like these, acting like gangsters. What are you doing here, anyway?'

'It's *my* island,' said Mr Eppy with a note of triumph in his voice. 'I've bought it. You can clear off – *when* I've found the way to the treasure with your help. Otherwise I shall have you arrested for trespassing and for trying to steal what is mine.'

'You're mad,' said Bill, in scorn. 'Absolutely crazy. I don't believe a word of it! You only heard of the island a day or two ago – you haven't had time to buy it. That's a wonderful tale – but you won't get *me* to believe it. Now, you keep your hands off all of us, and behave yourself – or you're the one that's going to land in prison and pretty quick too!'

Mr Eppy gave an order – and Bill was pounced on again by the three men. He was down on the ground in no time, and one of the men was tying his wrists and ankles together. Bill was strong, but his strength was no use against the three. Mr Eppy had Jack by the wrists so that he could not go to Bill's help, and as soon as Philip ran to help, he was struck by one of the men and sent spinning. Lucy-Ann began to cry with fright.

Lucian did nothing. He was trembling in a corner. Kiki and Micky were high up in a tree, watching in amazement. What was all this to-do? Kiki swooped down and gave Mr Eppy a nip on the ear again, and he nearly let Jack go, the pain was so sharp.

After Bill was tied up, the boys were tied too. 'Don't touch the girls,' threatened Bill. 'If you do you'll get more than you bargained for when we get out of here!'

It was no use. Dinah and Lucy-Ann were also tied up. Dinah was angry and mutinous, and Lucy-Ann was very frightened.

'And now,' said Mr Eppy, 'now *we* go to find the Andra treasure. *My* treasure! You had only the plan – I have the island, and I shall soon own the treasure! Thank you for showing me the way down!'

He went inside the column, and the three men followed him. Lucian was beckoned over and made to go down just behind his uncle. He looked very frightened.

'Well!' said Bill. 'Of all the scoundrels! Can we possibly get free whilst they're down there? It's our only chance!'

24

Prisoners!

Everyone waited till the last man had disappeared down the column. Then Bill spoke.

'Well, I'm blessed if I'll ever look at a treasure map again, or listen to anything you kids have to tell me! It's fatal. We plunge into trouble immediately. Jack, Philip – can you possibly loosen your ropes?'

'I've been trying,' said Philip, and Jack said the same. 'Those beasts know how to tie knots all right. The rope is biting into my ankles like anything, and I can hardly move my hands.'

All of them had their hands tied behind their backs, and it was really impossible to get free. Bill rolled himself over and over to the girls. He was very sorry for poor Lucy-Ann. Dinah was as tough as a boy, but Lucy-Ann could not help being scared.

'Lucy-Ann, don't be upset,' said Bill, ending up just by her. 'We'll think of some wonderful way to get even with these rogues.'

'I hope they'll get lost in the labyrinth,' said Jack fiercely, still struggling with the rope that tied his wrists.

'They probably will,' said Bill. 'In any case, they'll be a long time gone. We must somehow get free before they come back.'

'The first thing *I'll* do when I get free is to hop inside the column and get some of the food we put down there,' said Jack. 'That's if the brutes have left us any! I bet they've taken most of it with them.'

Bill privately thought they probably would have taken it, but he didn't say so. He gave up trying to loosen the rope round his wrists. It only made it cut into his flesh unbearably.

He looked round to see if there was a sharp stone he could perhaps rub his ropes on. He saw one and rolled over to it. But as his hands were behind his back he could not see what he was doing, and cut his fingers on the stone till they bled. He gave it up.

Kiki was up in the tree, muttering to herself. All the shouting and struggling had frightened her. She cocked her head down at Jack and decided it was safe to go to him. She flew down and landed on his middle.

'Send for the doctor,' she said, her head on one side. 'Send for the doctor, mistersir.'

'Good idea, Kiki,' said Jack, with an attempt at a grin. 'Tell him to come quickly! Telephone him at once!'

Kiki at once gave an imitation of a telephone bell

ringing. It sounded queer in that old ruined courtyard! Even Lucy-Ann gave a little laugh.

'Hello, hello!' said Kiki, pleased at the attention she was getting. 'Hello!'

'She's telephoning now!' grinned Jack. 'Good old Kiki. Got the doctor yet? Tell him we're all suffering from a nasty attack of Eppy-itis!'

Micky leapt down from the tree to join in the fun. He too had been badly scared, but now that everyone was talking and laughing, and the noisy men had gone, he felt safer. He landed on Philip, and tried to cuddle on to his shoulder. Philip was sitting up, his hands tied behind him.

'Sorry I can't stroke you, old thing, and make a bit of fuss of you after your scare,' said the boy. 'But my hands are tied! Yes, that's right – go and look for them. I've still got them – but they're behind me!'

Micky badly wanted to be nursed, but he could not find any arms to cuddle into! He went behind Philip to investigate. What had the boy done with his hands and arms? Ah – there they were behind him! Micky pulled at Philip's hands with his tiny paws. He wanted to be stroked and petted.

'Sorry, Micky – nothing doing,' said Philip. He grinned round at the others. 'Micky can't understand why I don't use my hands to pet him! He's pulling at them!'

Micky had discovered the rope that bound Philip's

wrists together. He was puzzled. What had Philip done with this rope? Why was it so tightly round the boy's hands? Micky tugged at the rope, and pulled at the knot.

Philip sat very still. 'That's right, Micky,' he said, in a caressing voice. 'That's right! You tackle those knots. Then I can pet you all you like!'

Everyone pricked up their ears at once. They looked eagerly at Philip. 'I say, Philip – is Micky – can Micky – do anything?'

'Don't know,' said Philip. 'He's fiddling about like anything. Go it, Micky. Pull those knots undone!'

But Micky couldn't. His tiny paws were not strong enough to undo the tightly tied knots of the rope. He gave it up. But he thought of something else!

He put his mouth down to the rope, and tried to gnaw it with his teeth!

'What *are* you doing, Micky?' cried Philip, feeling the wet little mouth against his wrist. 'Gosh, Bill, the clever little thing is trying to *gnaw* through the rope now!'

Everyone watched Philip intently. His face showed clearly all he was thinking. 'That's it, Micky – bite away!' he said. 'Good little monkey! No, go away, Kiki – don't interfere with Micky!'

Kiki had gone to Philip and was now getting behind him to see what Micky was up to. She watched him.

'One, two, three, GO!' she said, for all the world as if she was encouraging him.

'Come here, Kiki. Leave Micky alone in his good work,' ordered Jack, and Kiki came obediently.

'How's Micky getting on?' asked Bill.

'Fine, I think,' answered Philip, trying his hands to see if they felt any looser. 'I think the rope doesn't feel quite so tight. Go it, Micky.'

It was a long job, but Micky was patient and perservering. Once he knew that he was doing what Philip wanted, he went on and on. Bill marvelled at the way Philip understood animals and animals understood him. Any creature would do anything in the world for Philip!

'They're getting loose!' exclaimed Philip. 'Go on, Micky – just a bite or two more!'

And, sure enough, after another bout of patient gnawing, the rope snapped when Philip pulled on it. He brought his freed hands round to the front of him, groaning.

'My word – they're painful! Thanks, Micky, old thing – you did a very good job of work. Wait till my hands feel a bit better and I'll pat you from head to tail!'

The rope was still dangling from one of his wrists, the knots in it tied as tightly as ever. Philip picked it off with the other hand. He opened and shut his numb fingers, and then proceeded to pet the little monkey, who, delighted to be fussed, snuggled into Philip's arms with contented little grunts.

Nobody hurried Philip. Nobody begged him to be

quick and undo *their* bonds. Everyone knew that it was right for Micky to have his reward.

'Now, that's enough, old fellow,' said Philip at last. 'I must see to the others. You come and help!'

Philip put Micky on to his usual place on his shoulder. He felt in his pocket for a knife. His hands still felt queer and stiff, but they were rapidly getting more life into them. He brought out his knife and clicked it open.

He cut the rope round his ankles, and then he tried to stand up. His feet felt numb, for his ankles had been tied very tightly. But he was soon able to walk steadily. He went straight over to the girls.

He cut their bonds with his knife and Lucy-Ann gave a groan of thankfulness. 'Oh, Philip – thank you! That's better. Dinah, are your hands all right?'

'Bit stiff and numb,' said Dinah, rubbing them together. 'Wouldn't I like to tie up Mr Eppy! And wouldn't I make the ropes tight! The brute! He must be mad.'

Soon everyone was free. Bill found it hardest to stand because his ankles had been tied very viciously, and so had his hands. It took him some time to get the blood flowing freely in them, and it was a very painful process at first.

Everyone made a fuss of Micky, and the little monkey enjoyed it all thoroughly, chattering softly. Jack kept an eye on Kiki. She was jealous, and was looking out for a chance to nip Micky's long tail.

'I'll tie *you* up if you try any tricks, Kiki,' warned Jack, and tapped her smartly on the beak. She put her head under her wing, muttering to herself. 'Poor Polly, poor Polly, don't sniff, use your hanky!'

'She's irrepressible!' said Bill, still massaging his wrists. 'Well, I feel better now. What about some food, lads? *If* it's still there, of course!'

Jack was halfway to the column already. He had to get Philip to give him a good leg-up because his ankles still felt weak. Up he went, and dropped down inside. He looked about for the food. It was dark inside the column now, for the sun had gone. He felt about and, to his delight, found some bread and what felt like cheese. He called to Philip.

'Look out, Philip, I'm throwing the food out.'

Philip waited. Out came bread, cheese and a packet of some kind of meat. 'Wait a bit – here's some more bread,' shouted Jack, and out it came.

Jack climbed out again, grinning. 'They must have been in such a hurry to get to the treasure that they didn't even stop for a snack!' he said. 'They *must* have seen the food there.'

'Bill, is it safe to sit and have a meal?' asked Lucy-Ann anxiously.

'Quite safe,' said Bill. 'I'm going to sit here by the column and I shall be very, very sorry for anyone who tries to get out whilst *I'm* here!'

25

What happened in the night

It was getting quite dark now. The sun had gone a long time ago, and the children could hardly see one another as they sat together in the courtyard, munching hungrily.

'I've never known bread and cheese to taste so lovely,' said Dinah. 'Actually I didn't think this cheese was terribly nice yesterday – sort of sweetish – but today it's heavenly.'

'Only because you're so hungry,' said Jack, giving Kiki some of his. 'It's goat-milk cheese, isn't it, Bill? I say, look at Micky stuffing himself.'

'Pop goes Micky,' remarked Kiki, coming in at the right moment as usual. 'One, two, three, POP!'

'Idiot,' said Jack. 'Well, Bill – what are you thinking about?'

'Quite a lot of things,' said Bill soberly. 'We've had an extraordinary day. And I'm just planning what to do about it.'

'Wasn't that treasure wonderful!' said Lucy-Ann, her eyes shining.

Jack had, of course, heard all about their adventures underground by now, and was very envious because he was the only one who had not seen the treasure chamber, with its remarkable collection of riches. He had listened with amazement, and had wished and wished he had been with the others.

'What are your plans, Bill?' asked Philip, feeling that he could think sensibly again now that he was free and had had a good meal. 'I suppose we can't do much tonight.'

'No, we can't,' said Bill. 'That's quite certain. We've been through enough today without taking on any more adventures. Besides, the girls are nearly asleep, poor things!'

So they were. Excitement and exercise had completely tired them out. Lucy-Ann lay cuddled against Dinah, her eyes closed.

'Well, I'm pretty sleepy myself,' said Jack. He yawned loudly. 'I wouldn't mind a nice long snooze!'

'Anyway, Bill – what *could* we do, even if we *wanted* to do anything tonight?' asked Philip, beginning to yawn too. 'We can't escape! Andros won't come back, that's obvious, if Mr Eppy has threatened him with prison. After all, he's only an ordinary boatman! I expect Mr Eppy gave him plenty of money too, to make up for us not having paid him.'

'Yes – money and threats combined would soon send Andros away,' said Bill. 'In any case, Andros would know, of course, that Mr Eppy had his own boat here – possibly two boats, as he sent for more men and goods. So we shouldn't be absolutely stranded as Mr Eppy could always bring us back.'

'Gosh, yes – his boats must be *some*where, mustn't they?' said Philip, waking up considerably. 'We've only got to find them, Bill, and we're all right! Hadn't we better snoop round now, before the others come back from underground?'

'No. Nothing more tonight,' said Bill firmly. 'I've already planned to do that tomorrow. When we find Mr Eppy's boat or boats, we'll be all right, I hope. Now listen – I'm going to be on guard for the first four hours, and, after that, you, Jack, and then you, Philip, will have a two-hour watch, and by that time it will be morning.'

'What are we going to watch for? Are we to wait for dear old Eppy to pop his head out and say "Hello, there"?' asked Jack, with a grin.

'Exactly,' said Bill. He had now lighted one of the lanterns, and it gave a weird light to the scene. 'You two boys are tired – you won't be any good at watching till you've had a sleep. You can have your turn when I wake you.'

'Right,' said Jack, settling himself against Philip. 'We'll let the big tough guy watch first. As a matter of fact, I believe I'm asleep already.'

'What will you do if the others appear?' asked Philip, with interest. 'Knock them on the head as they come out of the hole?'

'Probably,' said Bill, and he lit his pipe. 'You don't need to worry about that. Good night! I'll wake you in four hours' time.'

The two boys were asleep almost before he had finished his sentence. The smell of Bill's tobacco wafted round the courtyard. Micky smelt it in his sleep and cuddled closer to Philip. He did not like the smell of tobacco. Kiki was standing on Jack, her head under her wing. The girls were absolutely still, sleeping soundly although they had such an uncomfortable resting place.

Bill put out the lantern. Only the glow of his pipe shone in the courtyard now and again. He was thinking hard. He went over all the happenings of the last two days. He considered Mr Eppy's assertion that the island was his. He puzzled over the whereabouts of the other creek, where probably Mr Eppy's boat or boats were. He wondered how the little party underground was getting on. He hoped fervently they were well and truly lost in the labyrinth.

He made his plans for the next day. They would find the boats. That would be the first thing. Where on earth would the creek be – the second creek that Andros had spoken about? Perhaps it would . . .

A noise stopped his thoughts at once. He put down his pipe and stood up, a silent figure close to the broken column. He listened. The noise had come from underground, he was sure of that.

Well – if it was the company coming back, he was in for a wakeful night! Bill picked up a large piece of wood that he had had his eye on all evening. It had probably been part of a door or window frame – now it would make a very good weapon!

He stood by the column, listening intently. A scraping noise came up to him – someone was climbing up the last part of the stone spiral. The noise stopped. The someone was evidently in the column now. What was he doing? He appeared to be feeling about for something. 'The food!' thought Bill, with a grin. 'Well – it's gone!'

A little whimper came up to him, and then a shaky voice said, in a low tone, 'Jack! Philip! Are you there?'

'Why – it's Lucian!' thought Bill in astonishment. 'Well – he can't be alone!'

He listened again. The whimpering began once more, rather like a miserable dog's. There was no sound of any other voice, or of anyone else coming up the stairway. Bill made up his mind. He leapt up to the broken edge of the hole in the column, switched on his torch and looked down.

Lucian was standing below him, his terrified face looking up, dirt caked on his cheeks. He put up his hand as if he expected Bill to aim a blow down at him.

'Lucian!' said Bill. 'What are you doing here? Where are the others?'

'I don't know,' moaned poor Lucian. 'They only took me down as far as that vault place at the bottom of these steps. They wouldn't let me go any further with them. They told me to stay there till they came back, and not to stir. My uncle said he'd half kill me if he didn't find me waiting for them when they came back.'

'Didn't they come back, then?' said Bill, keeping his torch on Lucian's face.

'No. And they went hours ago,' cried Lucian. 'I don't know what's happened to them. And I'm so hungry and cold and tired – and I'm frightened down there, too. I didn't dare to have my torch on all the time in case the battery gave out.'

Bill believed the frightened boy. 'Come on up,' he said. 'Here – take my hand and jump. Go on, Lucian, *jump*! Surely you can leap up here.'

Poor Lucian couldn't. In the end Bill had to get into the column and shove him up to the hole. Even then Lucian looked about to fall off. He was in a terrible state of nerves.

At last he was safely down in the courtyard, and Bill gave him some bread and cheese. He fell on it as if he hadn't eaten for a month.

A thought suddenly struck him. 'I say – how did you get free? I mean – weren't you all tied up?'

'Yes,' said Bill grimly. 'We were. But fortunately for you, we got free – yes, all of us. The boys are asleep over there, and the girls are nearby. No, don't wake them –

they're tired out. If we'd all been tied up still, you would have stayed in that column all night. Not a nice thought, Lucian!'

'No,' said Lucian, and shivered. 'I wish I hadn't come to this horrible island. What's going to happen? Are you going down to look for my uncle? He must be completely lost, you know.'

'He can stay lost, as far as I'm concerned,' said Bill. 'In fact, it will do him good. Your uncle is not a man I've any kindly feelings for, at present.'

'No. He's horrible,' agreed Lucian. 'Once he'd found the treasure he'd planned to leave you stranded here, all of you, and go off by himself to get more men to come and remove it.'

'Nice, thoughtful fellow,' said Bill. 'Well, young man, you'd better get some sleep. And tomorrow you're going to help us, to make up for the misdeeds of your nasty-minded uncle.'

'Oh – I'd be very glad to help you,' said Lucian at once. 'I would really. I'm on your side, you know that.'

'Yes, I expect you are,' said Bill. 'You'll have to be from now on, anyway!'

'How can I help you tomorrow?' asked Lucian.

'By taking us to the creek where your uncle's boats are,' said Bill at once.

'Oh, of course – if only I can remember where it is,' said Lucian anxiously. 'I'm not awfully good at remembering routes, you know. But I daresay I'll remember that.'

'You'll have to,' said Bill grimly. 'And now, go to sleep. No – don't go over to the boys. Just stay where you are. And mind – if your precious uncle arrives during the night, there's to be no warning to him from *you*. Otherwise some unpleasant things will happen to you.'

'Oh, I tell you I'm on *your* side now,' protested Lucian, and settled himself as comfortably as he could. 'Good night, sir. See you in the morning!'

26

Next morning

Four hours later Bill woke Jack. In a few sentences he told the surprised boy about the arrival of Lucian. 'He keeps saying he's on our side now, but you never know with a nitwit like that,' he warned Jack. 'So keep your eye on him. And if you hear the *slightest* sound from underground, prod me awake at once, Jack!'

'Right, Bill,' said Jack, fresh from his sound sleep. 'I say – they've been a long time underground, haven't they? They *must* be lost!'

'I sincerely hope so,' said Bill. 'I don't imagine they will be lost for ever, however desirable that might be – that labyrinth isn't a frightfully big one. Well, I'm going to sleep, Jack. Keep your wits about you!'

Jack was still sleepy. He was afraid he might find it difficult to keep awake, so he lit the lantern, and walked round the courtyard. He shone the light on to Lucian. He was so fast asleep that he did not even stir. Philip was soundly off too, and as for the girls, not an inch of their faces was to be seen, they were cuddled up so closely to one another.

Kiki accompanied Jack on his rambles round the courtyard. She knew she had to be quiet, so she whispered all the time. She wasn't very good at whispering, and tickled Jack's ear till he could not bear it any longer. He took her off his shoulder, and made her perch on one of his arms.

His two hours went by without anything happening at all. He woke Philip. It took a long time because the boy was so very sound asleep. As fast as Jack rolled him over to wake him, he rolled back again, his eyes still shut.

Jack took off one of Philip's shoes and tickled the soles of his feet. That woke him up all right! Philip sat straight up and glared round at the lantern Jack held.

'What are you . . .' he began, in a loud voice, and Jack shushed him at once.

'Shh, idiot! You'll wake the rest! Sorry about tickling your feet, but I simply *couldn't* wake you! It's your turn to watch now.'

Philip put on his shoe, saying something uncomplimentary to Jack under his breath. Micky woke up too, and looked in astonishment round the yard. He had forgotten where he was.

Jack told Philip in whispers about Lucian's arrival. Philip was amused. 'So Lucian is on our side now!' he said. 'Well – he's not a bad sort really – only he's *such* a nitwit! Poor Lucian – I guess he was scared out of his life!

Right, I'll keep my eye on him – though honestly he wouldn't have the nerve to do anything he shouldn't. And if our dear Mr Eppy pops his head up out of the column, I shall have the greatest pleasure in conking him good and hard.'

Jack grinned. 'Well, I'm off to sleep again,' he said. 'Good hunting, Philip!'

Philip's eyes persisted in closing, as he sat there keeping watch. He got up and walked about, as Jack had done. It would be an unforgivable thing to sleep while he was on guard. Quite unthinkable. He wondered what the time was, and glanced at his watch. The hands were phosphorescent, and showed him the time. Five o'clock – or getting on that way. He looked at the eastern sky. It was already silvering with the dawn.

It was almost at the end of Philip's two hours that the noise came. By this time the sun was up and the sunlight was on everything, clean and new and beautiful. Philip was enjoying the warmth of the first slanting beams when he heard the noise.

He pricked up his ears, and Micky began to chatter softly. 'Shh!' said Philip. 'I want to listen.' Micky was silent at once.

The noise came again – the scraping of boots on stone. They're coming! thought Philip, and he ran to where Bill was sleeping face down in the grass that grew over the yard. 'Bill! Wake up! They're coming!'

Bill woke up at once. He sprang to his feet, all sleep

gone in an instant. Jack awoke too, and so did the girls. Only Lucian slept on, but nobody took any notice of him.

Bill ran to the column. He took the big wedge of wood from Philip. 'Stand back,' he said to the girls. 'I don't expect for a moment I'll have much trouble, but you never know. I'm not standing any nonsense from Eppy and Co.'

He stationed himself just under the broken edge of the hole in the column. He listened. Voices came up to him. Someone was evidently now standing inside the column, having come up to the top of the spiral stairway. Bill heard what was said, but couldn't understand it.

However, he recognized Mr Eppy's voice, and took a firm hold of his piece of wood! Mr Eppy stood still for a moment and listened to someone shouting up to him from the stairway below. Then he called up in a low voice.

'Lucian? Are you there, Lucian?'

Lucian *was* there – but he was fast asleep, so of course he didn't answer. Mr Eppy called again softly. 'Lucian!'

Bill answered, in a grim voice. '*I'm* here – Bill Cunningham – and I'm waiting for you, Mr Eppy! The moment you try to get out of there I shall knock you back – with this weapon!' Bill banged his wedge of wood down on the column with such a noise that everyone jumped violently, and Lucian woke up.

There was a dead silence inside the column. Then

there was a scraping noise, as if someone else was coming up the stairway. Voices spoke together, very low.

'How did you get free?' came Mr Eppy's voice again. 'Did Lucian free you? He's not here.'

'No, he didn't,' said Bill.

The voices spoke together again. Then Mr Eppy called up urgently.

'Mr Cunningham! My men tell me that they have just found poor Lucian down here – badly hurt. He needs help. Let us come up at once.'

This was a most astonishing piece of news, especially to Lucian, whose mouth fell open in amazement. He was about to speak when Jack nudged him to be quiet. Bill was handling this!

'Sorry to hear that, Mr Eppy,' said Bill. 'Hand him up and we'll look after him. But you remain below. That's definite.'

Another conference took place in low voices. Then Mr Eppy spoke again.

'I must ask you to allow us to come up with the boy. He is seriously hurt. I am very distressed about him.'

Lucian's face was a study. Dinah almost giggled as she watched him. Bill answered at once.

'Nothing doing. Nobody comes up except, er, Lucian. Hand him over.'

As Lucian was even then sitting on the grass in the courtyard it was quite impossible for Mr Eppy to hand him over. Lucy-Ann whispered to Dinah, 'Isn't he a terrible storyteller!'

Bill began banging idly on the column with his wedge. 'Well, you don't seem to want to part with Lucian,' he called. 'Now I warn you – if anyone appears at the hole in this column they're for it!'

Bang, bang! That was Bill's piece of wood on the column again. It couldn't have pleased Mr Eppy very much. He was not a brave man, and it was easy to imagine his feelings down in the column!

'Can we have some food?' he called at last.

'No,' Bill shouted back hard-heartedly. 'There is barely enough for our breakfast.'

Judging by the scraping noises that could then be heard, Mr Eppy and the others had decided to go back down the stairs and have a conference. Bill jerked his head at Jack.

'Give out the food that's left to everyone. I'm staying here in case any of these fellows tries something funny. I have a feeling there's a revolver or two among them, so whatever happens I can't let them appear at the top.'

Jack and Philip shared out the remaining food. Bill gulped down his share, keeping eyes and ears open for any movement or sound from the broken column. But there was none.

He beckoned the others over to him at the end of the rather unsatisfactory meal. 'Now listen,' he said in a low voice. 'I must stay here, you can see that. What you have to do is to go with Lucian and find the creek where the boat or boats are, belonging to Mr Eppy. Be careful there are no men left in them.'

'There are two men with two boats,' said Lucian. This was disappointing news. Bill considered again.

'Well – the thing to do first of all is to find the creek with the boats,' said Bill. 'Don't show yourselves. Just find the creek so that we know the way. Then come back here. We'll hope that farm-boy arrives with more food at twelve o'clock, as he usually does.'

'We could do with it,' said Jack.

'So could our dear Mr Eppy and his friends,' grinned Philip. 'Bill, what do we do after we've found the creek and the boats, and come back to report?'

'We send Lucian down with a message supposedly from his uncle, to tell the men to come along up here,' said Bill, 'and we pop down and go off in the boats!'

'But, I say – you'll go on the rocks!' protested Lucian at once. 'You can't come to these islands without a boat-man who knows them. You'll be wrecked!'

This was a problem to be faced. Bill considered again.

'Well – we'll have to make up our minds about that when the time comes. In the meantime, off you go. Lucian, lead the way.'

Lucian, looking rather doubtful, went to the sloping city street. He set off down it, and turned off to the left halfway down.

'You seem to know the way, all right,' said Jack approvingly. Lucian looked at him uneasily.

'I don't,' he said. 'I'm absolutely no good at this kind of thing. I can never can find my way anywhere. I've no sense of direction at all. I shall *never* find the boats!'

27

Unexpected visitors

Lucian was perfectly right. He did not know the way, and he could not find the boats. He was completely hopeless. He simply wandered here and there, making towards the sea, but arriving at a rocky beach where no boats could possibly lie.

'You're a mutt,' said Jack in disgust.

'Mutt!' said Kiki, pleased with the word. 'Mutty! Send for the doctor.'

Nobody smiled even at this. They were all too disappointed and disgusted with poor Lucian. He looked ready to cry.

'It's not my fault,' he said with a sniff. 'If I'd known it was going to be so important I'd have taken careful note of the way. But I didn't know.'

'Now, look here – if you start to moan again I'll push you down a rabbit hole, and stuff it up with seaweed,' said Jack in disgust. Lucian looked alarmed.

'I *would* remember if I could,' he said dismally. 'But I

do tell you this – nobody can come or go from these islands in a boat without a seaman who knows the way. There are hundreds of rocks just below the surface of the sea. Even an experienced seaman finds it difficult. I know because I've so often visited them with my uncle.'

Jack looked at him. 'Well – I believe you about that,' he said. 'I shouldn't care to navigate a boat myself without a sailor who knew the way. Gosh – we're really beaten now – no boats – and if we had them we'd probably wreck ourselves. A very poor outlook indeed!'

Lucy-Ann immediately had a vision of them and Mr Eppy and his friends remaining on Thamis Island for years and years! She sighed.

'I wish I'd never bought that ship in a bottle for Philip,' she said. 'If I'd known it was going to bring us such an adventure I'd have thrown it away!'

They began to make their way back to the city. As they went, Jack stopped and looked up at the sky. 'What's that noise?' he said. 'Sounds like an aeroplane!'

They all stopped then and listened, looking for the plane. Soon it came into sight, a small speck coming in from the north.

'Pity we can't make a signal of distress,' said Dinah. 'Anyway, I'm going to wave my hanky!'

She took out a small hanky and, much to the others' amusement, waved it wildly in the air.

'Do you really suppose for one moment that the

plane can see your dirty little hanky, and would come down here if it did?' demanded Philip.

'You never know,' said Dinah, still waving vigorously.

'You're daft,' said Philip, and Dinah gave him one of her best scowls. Leaving her waving madly, the others went on, still keeping an eye on the plane, which by now was over the island. It flew over it – and then made a wide circuit and flew back!

'It's seen my hanky!' shrieked Dinah. 'It's coming back!'

'Don't be an ass,' said Philip. But the plane certainly had come back – and what was more, it was coming down low too, making another circuit of the whole island as it flew.

'There's a flat space over there. Look! Look!' screamed Dinah to the plane, as if she really thought it could hear her. 'Come down there! Oh, don't pass it!'

The plane swooped down still lower and came round again. It seemed to see the flat place that Dinah had yelled about, and it came down neatly, as slowly as it could. Its wheels touched the ground, and for one awful moment it looked as if the rough ground was going to tip the plane over on its nose. But it righted itself and came to a stop.

Dinah looked at the others with flushed cheeks. 'There you are! It saw my hanky – and it heard my yell!'

The others were staring in delight at the plane. 'It

can't be friends of Mr Eppy's!' cried Philip. 'It must be someone sent to look for us. Come on!'

Their feet flew along over the rough paths. They saw two men getting out of the plane. They waved to the children and went to meet them.

Lucy-Ann's sharp eyes recognized them first. 'It's TIM!' she squealed. 'Tim, Bill's friend. And isn't that Andros the boatman with him?'

She was right. It *was* Tim, and beside him was a rather shamefaced Andros. Tim hailed them.

'Hello, hello! Where's Bill? Are you all safe? Andros here came to me with such a wild story I had to come along and investigate!'

'Yes, Bill's all right!' cried Jack, and he pumped Tim's arm up and down in sheer delight at seeing him. 'I say, it's good to see you. Did Andros really come and tell you about us?'

'He told me a most extraordinary tale,' said Tim. 'He apparently chewed it over for a day or so, and then decided he'd better tell someone. When he saw me down at the quayside, trying to spot you all, he recognized me and came up. He said that he took you to Thamis and dropped you there. Then he fell asleep waiting for you.'

'That's right,' said Jack.

'And then someone came and woke him up in a hurry, and told him he'd no right to be there, and threatened him with prison,' said Tim. 'Andros replied that he'd left a party there, a man and four children, a parrot and a monkey – and this fellow raved at him, said it was his own island, and if Andros didn't clear out then and there he'd have him arrested straight away.'

'Mr Eppy in a rage, evidently,' said Jack.

'Andros then pointed out that he hadn't been paid and this fellow poured money into his hands and then pointed a revolver at him. So Andros fled, comforting himself by thinking that as the fellow had a boat some-where he could at least bring you all off in his own good time. That right, Andros?'

'I do not understand all, Mister, sir,' said Andros. 'Bad man here. Very bad. Andros very sorry, Mister, sir.'

'Well, now *you* tell your tale,' said Tim to Jack. So between them the children poured out their story – and it was such an astonishing one that Tim listened open-mouthed. Good gracious – what a tale! He had never heard anything like it in his life.

He soon grasped everything, and grinned to think of old Bill standing patiently by the broken column, wait-ing for Mr Eppy or his men to come out and be dealt with.

'I wouldn't mind dealing with them myself,' said the young man cheerfully. 'Biff, thud, ker-plonk – very nice too!'

'Oh, Tim – you do make me laugh!' said Lucy-Ann with a giggle. 'I wonder if Bill has been doing any biffing.'

'Well, if he has, I hope it's Mr Eppy that's getting the

biffs, to say nothing of the ker-plonks,' said Tim, grinning. 'Well, now – what's our plan to be?'

'We've got to find the other creek and the boats,' said Jack. 'That's the first thing to do. Then we've got to get the two men out of the way – the ones who are with the boats. Then somehow we've got to get the boats going and sail off safely without being wrecked on the rocks.'

'Well, Andros will know where the creek is – in fact, I know myself,' said Tim. 'I saw it from the plane – and saw the boats there too. And Andros and I will see to the two men all right.'

'No. We know a better way than that to get them out of the way,' said Philip, and he told Tim his plan to send Lucian to them with a fake message. Tim nodded.

'Yes, that's better, really. Saves a lot of rough stuff. Not that I mind that, but I'm not sure about our friend here. He's not made of such stern stuff as he might be.'

'I think we'd better get back and see Bill before we do anything,' said Jack. 'And anyway, we don't want to get the two boatmen out of the way yet, and turn them on to old Bill. That wouldn't be a very good plan. Come on – let's get back to Bill.'

So off they all went, Kiki chattering merrily, knowing that the children were now feeling very much more cheerful. 'Mistersir,' she said to Andros. 'Mistersir, mister!'

They got back to the temple courtyard, and Bill stared in surprise to see Tim. 'Hello!' he said. 'Well, well,

well – so it *was* your plane I saw coming over the island. I couldn't see it come down from here, but I hoped it had. Bit of luck you meeting with the children. I suppose they've told you all the news.'

'Yes, rather,' grinned Tim. 'Pretty adventurous lot, aren't you? Any trouble with the chappies down the column?'

'Just a biff or two a little while ago,' said Bill. '*Not* on Mr Eppy's head, unfortunately – one of the other fellows, I fear. I haven't heard so much as the flick of an eyelid since.'

The sound of a bell came echoing up the ruined street. 'Dong-dong-dong!'

'Pussy's down the well!' screeched Kiki, suddenly remembering ding-dong-bell. 'Who put her in, who put her in?'

'What on earth's that bell?' asked Tim, startled. 'Are we late for school or what?'

'Don't be silly!' said Lucy-Ann, laughing. 'That's our food. It comes every day regularly at this time. And I'm jolly glad – I'm still hungry after our poor breakfast.'

Tim was amazed to see the imp of a boy coming along with the panniered donkey. Bill did not leave his post by the column, but handed out money to Jack to pay for the food. The boy emptied the panniers, winked at Tim and spat once more at Micky. The monkey immediately spat back, and his aim was a lot better than the boy's. 'Pah!' said the little imp in disgust.

'Pah!' echoed Kiki. 'Pooh! Dong-dong-dong, pop goes the pah!'

The boy gave her a look of amazement and climbed on his donkey's back. He sent a stream of comments at Kiki, who copied him at once, ending with one of her pistol shots. The donkey reared in fright, and then galloped off with the boy at top speed.

'You'll be the death of me one day, Kiki,' said Bill, weak with laughing. 'Now then – hand out the food, Jack – and I suppose we'd better throw a bit down the column, or our friends below will starve to death!'

Fortunately the boy had brought a great deal of food, so there was plenty for everyone. Bill yelled down the column in a stentorian voice:

'If you want food, there's some coming. But don't try any funny tricks, or you won't get any more!'

Somebody evidently came up to get the bread, cheese and meat that Bill threw down. He also threw some fruit, feeling that the men must be as thirsty as he was. There was no word of thanks from anyone in the column, and no sound after the food had been taken.

'Wonder if they found the treasure,' said Jack, munching hard. 'Wish I'd seen it! I bet I shan't now – and if I don't, it'll be the disappointment of my life!'

28

Escape!

Plans were made while they ate. 'Tim, I want you to take the two girls off in your plane,' said Bill. 'I don't want anyone exposed to danger here one moment longer than necessary. Andros, once we have got rid of the two men down in the boats, you are to take charge of the better boat of the two, and go off with the rest of us.'

'What, Bill? Do you mean to say we're going to leave a boat for those scoundrels to escape in?' cried Jack indignantly.

'No. I'm going to ask Andros if he will kindly remove some small thing from the engine of the other boat so that it won't start up when the men want it to,' said Bill with a laugh. 'I think it would be a very good thing to leave them here, prisoners, till we report them, and find out whether Mr Eppy has bought the island or not. If he has, he's in a strong position of course, and nothing we say will be listened to with much attention.'

'He's always buying and selling islands,' put in

Lucian. 'I expect he has bought this all right. He's well known for that.'

'You may be right,' said Bill. 'Do you want to come with us, Lucian, or stay and welcome your uncle out of the column?'

There was no doubt about what Lucian wanted to do. He was going with Bill and the others!

They all felt a lot better after the meal. Tim set off for the plane with the two girls, who hugged Bill before they went and begged him to keep himself safe.

'I shan't set off in the plane till I hear your motor boat starting up and going off,' said Tim. 'Goodbye for the present. Come on, girls. What people are going to say when I land with you at the airport I cannot imagine. You're too dirty for anything – regular little grubs!'

Andros, Lucian, Jack and Philip set off for the boats. It was decided that only Lucian should go right up to the boats and give the false message. He was to say that the men were wanted up in the temple courtyard, and give them directions as to how to get there. As soon as Bill spotted them coming he was to leave the broken column where he was on guard, and go to the boats, keeping himself out of sight of the two men.

'Then we'll be into one of the boats in a jiffy, and off and away!' said Jack joyfully. 'That will show Mr Eppy!'

Andros led the way. He knew the other creek well, though he did not consider it as good as the one he had landed in. When they got near to the boats, Lucian went on alone, while the others hid themselves behind bushes.

Lucian was nervous but tried not to show it. He went up to the boats and shouted loudly. 'Ahoy there – where are you?'

The two men appeared. Lucian began to say something loudly in Greek, and the two men nodded. They leapt from the boat to the beach, and made their way up the shore. Lucian was telling them where to go, pointing this way and that.

'Well, I hope he's telling them correctly,' thought Jack, remembering how hopeless Lucian had been at trying to find the way to the boats that morning. 'Let's hope he has been more careful at marking the way this time.'

The men soon disappeared. Andros raced to the boats. He chose the smaller one of the two as being the better. He went to the other boat and tinkered with the engine. He withdrew something from it and threw it into the other boat, where it fell with a thud.

He grinned at the boys. 'That boat no good now,' he said. 'Engine dead. We get in here quick.'

They all got in. Andros tinkered about with the engine there too. It started up quickly and he stopped it at once.

The boys wondered how old Bill was getting on. Had he spotted the two boatmen? Was he even now coming down to the boat, keeping himself unseen? They hoped so.

Suddenly they heard shouts, and they all sat up straight in their boat. What was that?

Bill was tearing down to the shore at top speed. Behind him were the two men, also running at top speed. Andros acted quickly. He started up the engine at once, and called to the boys to give a hand to Bill when he came.

Red in the face and panting hard, Bill raced up to the boat. Willing hands dragged him in, and almost as he touched the deck of the boat it was off and away, its engine making a terrific noise in the calm of the little creek.

The two men leapt into the other boat at once, shouting angrily. Andros gave a malicious grin. Bill saw it and knew what it meant. The other boat was useless!

No amount of trying would make the second boat start up. Its engine was dead. The two men realised that Andros must have tampered with it, and they stood up, shaking their fists and shouting unintelligibly. Jack and Philip enjoyed it all thoroughly, but poor Lucian was as white as a sheet.

'Well – we're off,' said Bill, getting his breath again. 'Gosh, I had a narrow escape. I was watching for the men, but they came on me unawares. They must have guessed there was some trickery about, because they suddenly made a bee-line for me and gave me a jolly hard run. I was glad I'd got all directions from Andros as to where the creek was. I nearly missed my way as it was.'

'Any sound from Eppy and Co.?' asked Jack. Bill shook his head.

'No, but they'll have heard the shouts and I expect they'll be out of the column by now and having a good snoop round. They'll join up with the other two men and then Mr Eppy will have a few choice things to say to the two men who left the boats, and so gave us the means of escape. I expect he is thinking of quite a lot of things to say to Lucian too, for giving them that fake message.'

Lucian gave a feeble smile. He was still very white. 'I shall get a fearful beating,' he said.

'You won't,' said Bill. 'I'll see to that. I'll give your uncle something to think about, when I get back to the airport island. He's going to find himself in hot water very, very soon. I don't care whether he's bought the island or not. He's a rogue.'

The sound of an aeroplane's engine attracted their attention. 'It's Tim's plane!' cried Jack, and he stood up in the motor-boat and waved. 'Ahoy there, Tim!'

The plane swooped down low, and Kiki gave a squawk of terror. Micky hid his head under Philip's arm. The boys cheered and yelled. 'Good-bye, good luck, Tim! Hello there, girls.'

At about six o'clock in the evening the motor-boat arrived at the airport island. The first thing they saw was the *Viking Star* in the harbour, still lying silent. The second thing they saw was Tim on the quayside – and the girls with him! They had landed a long time ago, had

had a good meal, and then had come down to the quay to wait for the others.

'I've been to the police,' said Tim. 'Told the chief you had something to report and would he please not go home till he'd seen you. He's all hot and bothered – it isn't often anything happens here!'

Bill laughed. 'Well, I expect the report will really have to go to the mainland to be dealt with – but as Andros comes from here, and Mr Eppy hired his boats from here, and presumably saw lawyers here if he bought the island, it's best to see the chief of police of this island.'

The chief was a small bird-like man with an intelligent face, and quick, darting eyes. He spoke English very well. He was very thrilled to think there might be some important news for him.

He listened intently to Bill's remarkable story, asking a few questions now and again. The children added little bits. When the inspector heard of the treasure he almost fell off his chair.

'We must find out if this man Eppy did buy the island,' he said. 'I know him. He is always buying islands and selling them. I do not like him. He is crazy.'

A good deal of telephoning then went on, with a few 'Hallos' from a rather bored Kiki, and some 'Mistersirs' and 'One, two, three, pops!'

At last the little man turned to Bill, his face beaming.

'Paul Eppy *did* try to buy the island. But it is not for sale. It is not his – it belongs to our government.'

'*Good!*' said all the children together.

'What a nerve Mr Eppy has!' said Dinah.

'I hope he will not get away with any of that unique treasure,' said the inspector. 'He is not an honest man.'

'He can't,' said Jack, with a grin. 'Andros tampered with the only motor boat there – he can't use it. He's a prisoner there, and so are all the rest of them.'

'Good. I think that is *very* good,' beamed the bird-like man. He turned to Bill. 'If you will be kind enough to put in a report, sir – a detailed one – for me to forward to the mainland – I would be very much obliged. The children should read it, and sign it. And Andros here should sign the part of it that refers to his doings in the matter.'

'Right,' said Bill, and got up to go. 'Well, that's that. I've had some thrilling adventures with these four – but this beats the lot. I only wish we could have a bit of that treasure!'

'Sir, you shall,' said the inspector earnestly. 'I will see to it personally. My government will be very honoured to allow you to choose what you want from it.'

'A carved dagger for me!' said Philip, at once. 'Gosh, what would the chaps at school say!'

'Come along,' said Bill. 'We'll go on board the *Viking Star*, and take Tim to dinner there with us. I want a good bath, a good shave, a good meal and a good sleep in a comfortable bed.'

And off they all went on board the *Viking Star*, happy and excited, talking nineteen to the dozen!

29

Happy ending after all!

In the night the *Viking Star* sailed once more. Bill did not hear the engines starting up, nor did any of the five children. Kiki woke up, poked her head out from under her wing and then put it back again.

It was astonishing to find themselves at sea again. They were making for Italy. 'Oh dear – we've left the treasure island far behind,' said Lucy-Ann mournfully.

'Don't be a humbug,' said Jack. 'You know you're jolly glad you escaped from it.'

'Yes, I know that,' said Lucy-Ann. 'But I just hate leaving all that treasure.'

'I never even saw it,' Jack reminded her. 'I feel I've been done out of something – all because that idiot of a Kiki took it into her head to fly off my shoulder just as we were going to look for the treasure. Nitwit!'

'Nit-wit,' echoed Kiki pleasantly. 'Tit-bit!' She flew down and looked at a plate of grapes.

'No, you don't,' said Jack, and removed it from her.

'No titbits for a nitwit – and anyway, you've helped your-self to about two hundred grapes already. You're a greedy pig, Kiki.'

'I suppose the rest of this cruise will be as dull as ditchwater,' said Philip. He glanced at the little carved ship on the dressing table of his cabin. 'Golly – weren't we thrilled when we found the treasure map inside! Bill says we've got to give that up to the Greek museum, but we can keep the re-drawn map, the one we used – if we can get it back from Mr Eppy!'

'I wonder what Mother will say to all this,' said Dinah suddenly. 'She won't be a bit pleased with Bill, will she? She'll never speak to him again!'

'Well – that would mean we'd never even *see* him again!' said Lucy-Ann, horrified at the thought. 'I simply love Bill. I wish he was my father. It's horrid not having a father or a mother. You're lucky, you and Philip, Dinah, you *have* got a mother, even if you haven't a father.'

'Well, you share our mother with us, don't you?' said Philip at once. 'You call her Aunt Allie – and she treats you as if she was your mother.'

'Yes, I know. She's a darling,' said Lucy-Ann, and said no more. She was worrying about Bill. Suppose Aunt Allie really kept her word, and refused to speak to Bill again because he had taken them into danger? That really would be dreadful.

It was maddening to sail away from all the romantic little islands, just as they had had such an adventure – all

260

the children longed to know what had happened after they had left. What did Mr Eppy do? What happened to him? How did he eventually get off the island – or was he still there? And what about the treasure, that fabulous, amazing treasure hidden in the round treasure chamber deep down in the heart of the old ruined city?

Bill promised to let them know all he heard – and he was as curious as the children! The *Viking Star* put in at Naples, and then went on to Spain. It was there that Bill got the first news. He came straight to the children.

'Well, you'll be glad to know that Eppy and Co. couldn't get off the island, and almost went mad with rage about it. Then that police inspector chap sent a boat there – and what's more went in it himself – and had the whole lot arrested then and there. What a shock for Mr Eppy!'

'What about the treasure?' asked Dinah eagerly.

'It's all been brought out of the round rock-chamber, and is being sent to the mainland to be examined and valued. A list of the things will be sent to us – and we are each to choose a memento!'

'Gosh!' said Jack. 'I'll have a dagger, like Philip, then. I bet the girls will have jewellery.'

'*Is* it the Andra treasure?' asked Lucy-Ann.

'They seem to think so,' said Bill. All their eyes went to the little ship on the dressing table. There it stood, its sails set, its Greek name showing on its side. The *Andra*. What a Ship of Adventure it had been!

'What's going to happen about Lucian?' asked Dinah. Lucian was still on the *Viking Star*, but with *them*, not with his aunt and uncle this time! His aunt, in hysterical tears, had remained on the airport island to be with her husband. Bill had offered to take Lucian back to England, and park him with a school friend till it was time for him to return to his school.

'Lucian is to go to other relations in future for the holidays,' said Bill. 'That is, unless *we* can occasionally put up with him. I feel sorry for that lad.'

There was a silence. 'It's awful when you feel you've got to do something you don't like doing just because you're sorry for someone,' said Lucy-Ann with a sigh. 'I don't know whether Aunt Allie will like to have him, anyway. And oh, Bill – do you think she's going to be very cross with you about all this? This adventure, I mean?'

'Yes. I think she is,' said Bill. 'I telephoned her from Italy, and told her a little. Perhaps I should have waited till we saw her. She wasn't at all pleased.'

'Oh, dear – we shan't have a very nice time the rest of the hols,' said Lucy-Ann. 'I don't like it when Aunt Allie is upset or cross. She'll be tired, too, after looking after her Aunt Polly. I do wish this adventure was going to have a nice end, not a nasty one!'

Everyone was quite glad when at last the *Viking Star* arrived at Southampton at the end of her long cruise. After the exciting adventure in the middle of it, things had seemed very tame and dull. It was lovely to be on firm land again, going home. Mrs Mannering was not going to meet them. She was leaving her aunt the day before and going home to get things ready for the family. Lucian was to be left with a school friend of his on the way. They were all going home in Bill's car.

The boy was sad to say goodbye when the time came. He stammered and stuttered as he held out his hand to each of them in turn. 'Goodbye – er – I do hope I'll s-s-see you all again. I've had – er – er – a lovely time – and er – I'm sorry for anything I did you didn't like – and – er . . .'

'Er-er-er,' copied Kiki in delight. 'Pah! Send for the doctor. Er-er-er-er-er-er . . .'

'Shut up, Kiki, and behave yourself,' said Jack, vexed. But Lucian didn't mind.

'I shall miss old Kiki,' he said. 'And Micky, too. Goodbye, Micky – er – think of me sometimes, all of you.'

He almost ran from them, and Lucy-Ann stared after him, rather distressed. 'Poor old Lucian – he was almost crying,' she said. 'He's really rather a nice old – er – nice old . . .'

'Nit-wit,' said everyone, and Kiki yelled out too. 'NIT-WIT! Send for the doctor!'

'Well, he's nice for a nitwit, then,' said Lucy-Ann. She settled down in the car again. 'Now for home – and dear old Aunt Allie. I've got a frightfully big hug saved up for her!'

Mrs Mannering was delighted to see them all, though she was rather cool to Bill. She had a wonderful tea ready for them, and Kiki screeched with delight to see a plate laid for her and Micky, with a lovely fruit salad.

'One, two, three, GO!' she said, and settled down to eat, keeping an eye on Micky's plate, hoping she could snatch a titbit from it.

After tea they all sat in the comfortable sitting room, and Bill lit his pipe. He looked rather gloomy, the children thought.

'Well, Allie,' he began. 'I suppose you want to hear it all – the hunt for the Andra treasure – and all that happened.'

'We had some jolly narrow escapes,' said Jack, stroking Kiki. 'And you'll be glad to know, Aunt Allie, that Kiki got two grand nips at Mr Eppy's ear!'

They began their tale. Mrs Mannering listened in amazement. Her eyes went continually to the little carved ship on the mantelpiece, put proudly there by Philip as soon as he reached home.

'There!' said Philip when they had finished their tale. 'What do you think of that?'

Mrs Mannering did not answer. She looked at Bill. He would not meet her eyes, but knocked out his pipe very hard on the fender.

'Oh, Bill,' said Mrs Mannering sadly. 'You promised me – and you broke your word. I shall never trust you again. You promised faithfully not to lead the children into any kind of adventure again. I wouldn't have asked you to look after them if I hadn't trusted you. I can't trust you any more'

'Aunt Allie! What do you *mean*, you can't trust Bill any more?' cried Lucy-Ann indignantly, and she went to Bill and put her arms round him. 'Can't you see he's the nicest, most trustable person in the whole world?'

Mrs Mannering could not help laughing. 'Oh, Lucy-Ann – you're very fierce, all of a sudden. It's just that every time I leave you alone with Bill you get into horrible danger. You know you do.'

'Well, why can't you and Bill always be with us together?' demanded Lucy-Ann. 'I don't see why you can't *marry* each other – then we'd always have Bill, and you could keep an eye on him to see he doesn't lead us into adventures.'

Bill exploded into an enormous shout of laughter. Mrs Mannering smiled broadly. The others looked at one another.

'I say!' said Philip eagerly, 'that's a wizard idea of Lucy-Ann's! We'd have a father then – all of us! Gosh, fancy having Bill for a father. Wouldn't the other boys envy us?'

Bill stopped laughing and looked soberly round at the four beaming children. Then he looked at Mrs Mannering. He raised his eyebrows enquiringly.

'Well, Allie?' he said in a curiously quiet voice. 'Do *you* think it's a good idea, too?'

She looked at him, and then smiled round at the eager children. She nodded. 'Yes – it's really a very good idea, Bill. I'm surprised we've never thought of it before!'

'That's settled, then,' said Bill. 'I'll take these four kids on – and you'll see to it I don't lead them into any more adventures, Allie. Is that agreed?'

'*Well!* This adventure had a wonderful ending after all!' said Lucy-Ann, drawing a deep breath. Her eyes shone like stars. 'Good old Bill! Oh, I'm so happy now!'

'God save the Queen,' said Kiki excitedly. 'Polly put the doctor on, send for the kettle. Pop goes Bill!'

How well do you know *The Ship of Adventure*?
Take this quiz to find out!

1. What is the name of the ship that the children go on
   holiday in in *The Ship of Adventure*?

a. Lucky Star
b. Falling Star
c. Viking Star
d. Shooting Star

2. What was the first stop on the trip?

a. Lisbon
b. Madrid
c. Paris
d. Crete

3. What do the children name Philip's pet monkey?

a. Lizzie
b. Ernest
c. Micky
d. Cheeky

4. What does Philip really want that Lucy then gets him for his birthday?

a. A monkey

b. A pet rat

c. A new wallet

d. A ship in a bottle

5. Who broke the ship in the bottle?

a. Lucy-Ann

b. Kiki and Micky

c. Kiki

d. Micky

6. Why does Bill come to join the children?

a. He got some unexpected time off work

b. Mrs Mannering had to fly home to see her ill aunt

c. He was worried about the children

d. He needed a holiday

7. What is the name of the island marked on the old treasure map that the children and Bill go to explore?

a. Thamis

b. Crete

c. Puffin Island

d. The Isle of Gloom

8. Who runs away in the underground tunnels?

a. Micky
b. Lucy-Ann
c. Kiki
d. Philip's dormouse

9. What do Mrs Mannering and Bill decide to do in the last chapter of *The Sea of Adventure*?

a. Send the children to boarding school
b. Open a hotel
c. Go on holiday
d. Get married

10. What is the name of the next book in the Adventure series?

a. The Circus of Adventure
b. The River of Adventure
c. The Valley of Adventure
d. The Mountain of Adventure

How well did you do?
Answers below!

ANSWERS: 1 c; 2 a; 3 c; 4 d; 5 b; 6 b; 7 a; 8 c; 9 d; 10 a

Philip, Jack, Dinah, Lucy-Ann and Kiki the parrot have been on another exciting adventure.

Can you find all the words from the story in the wordsearch below?

T	S	T	H	A	M	I	S	B	C	P
V	T	H	J	L	A	S	E	F	E	A
L	I	W	I	C	R	L	R	S	T	S
N	Q	K	E	P	R	A	U	L	H	S
D	O	S	I	G	I	N	S	I	N	P
A	Q	T	P	N	A	D	A	S	A	O
M	F	G	P	K	G	S	E	B	I	R
R	F	T	D	M	E	S	R	O	C	T
E	E	V	I	O	A	K	T	N	U	V
P	A	C	G	N	N	H	Q	A	L	D
P	K	V	D	K	D	T	T	G	R	K
Y	J	N	N	E	R	C	C	U	M	N
V	D	G	E	Y	A	W	X	Q	O	K
K	D	V	G	R	E	E	K	F	B	S

Ship
Southampton
Viking Star
Passport
Lisbon

Thamis
Micky
Monkey
Lucian
Mr Eppy

Andra
Treasure
Islands
Greek
Marriage

Don't miss . . .

The
Circus of
ADVENTURE

the next exciting book in Enid Blyton's
thrilling Adventure series

1

Home from school

The quiet house was quiet no longer! The four children were back from boarding school, and were even now dragging in their trunks, shouting to one another. Kiki the parrot joined in the general excitement, of course, and screeched loudly.

'Aunt Allie! We're back!' yelled Jack. 'Be quiet, Kiki! I can't hear myself shout!'

'Mother! Where are you?' called Dinah. 'We're home again!'

Her mother appeared in a hurry, smiles all over her face. 'Dinah! Philip! I didn't expect you quite so soon. Well, Lucy-Ann, you've grown! And Philip, you look bursting with health!'

'I don't know why,' grinned Philip, giving Mrs Cunningham a big hug. 'The food at school is so frightful I never eat any of it!'

'Same old story!' said Mrs Cunningham, laughing. 'Hallo, Kiki! Say how do you do!'

'How do you do?' said the parrot, solemnly, and held out her left foot as if to shake hands.

'New trick,' said Jack. 'But wrong foot, old thing. Don't you know your left from your right yet?'

'Left, right, left, right, left, right,' said Kiki at once, and began marking time remarkably well. 'Left, right, left . . .'

'That's enough,' said Jack. He turned to Mrs Cunningham. 'How's Bill? Is he here too?'

'He meant to be here to welcome you all,' said Mrs Cunningham, Bill's wife. 'But he had a sudden 'phone call this morning, took the car, and went racing off to London all in a hurry.'

The four children groaned. 'It isn't some job that's turned up just as we're home for the Easter hols, is it?' said Lucy-Ann. 'Bill's always got some secret work to do just at the wrong time!'

'Well, I hope it isn't,' said Mrs Cunningham. 'I'm expecting him to telephone at any moment to say if he's going to be back tonight or not.'

'Mother! Shall we unpack down here and take our things up straight away?' called Dinah. 'Four trunks lying about the hall leave no room to move.'

'Yes. But leave two of the trunks downstairs when they're empty,' said her mother. 'We're going off on a holiday tomorrow, all of us together!'

This was news to the children. They clustered round Mrs Cunningham at once. 'You never said a word in your letters! Where are we going? Why didn't you tell us before?'

'Well, it was really Bill's idea, not mine,' said Mrs Cunningham. 'He just thought it would make a nice change. I was surprised myself when he arranged it.'

'Arranged it! And never said a word to us!' said Philip. 'I say – is anything up? It seems funny that Bill did it all of a sudden. Last time I saw him, when he came down to school to see us, he was talking about what we'd all do at *home* in the four weeks' Easter hols.'

'I don't really think there's anything *peculiar* about it,' said his mother. 'Bill gets these sudden ideas, you know.'

'Well – where are we all going to, then?' asked Jack, pushing Kiki off the sideboard, where she was trying to take the lid off the biscuit jar.

'It's a place called Little Brockleton,' said Mrs Cunningham. 'Very quiet. In the middle of the country. Just the kind of place you all like. You can mess about in old things all day long.'

'Little *Brock*leton,' said Philip. 'Brock means badger. I wonder if there are badgers there. I've always wanted to study badgers. Lovely little bear-like beasts.'

'Well, *you*'ll be happy then,' said Dinah. 'I suppose that means you'll be keeping a couple of badgers for pets before we know where we are! Ugh!'

'Badgers are very nice animals,' began Philip. 'Clean and most particular in their habits, and . . .'

4

Lucy-Ann gave a little squeal of laughter. 'Oh dear – they don't sound a *bit* like you then, Philip!'

'Don't interrupt like that and don't make silly remarks,' said Philip. 'I was saying, about badgers . . .'

But nobody wanted to listen. Jack had a question he wanted to ask. 'Are there any decent birds round about Little Brockleton?' he said. 'Where *is* it? By the sea?'

Jack was as mad as ever about birds. So long as he could do birdwatching of some kind he was happy. Mrs Cunningham laughed at him.

'You and your birds, Jack, and Philip and his badgers! I can't tell you anything about the birds there – the same ones as usual, I suppose. Now – what about these trunks? We'll unpack the lot; take the boys' trunks upstairs, and leave the girls' to take with us to Little Brockleton – they are not *quite* so hard-used as yours!'

'Can we have something to eat after we've unpacked?' asked Philip. 'I'm famished. The school food, you know, is so . . .'

'Yes – I've heard all that before, Philip,' said his mother. 'You'll have a fine lunch in half an hour – yes, your favourite – cold meat, salad, baked beans in tomato sauce, potatoes in their jackets, heaps of tomatoes . . .'

'Oh, good!' said everyone at once, and Kiki hopped solemnly from one leg to another.

'Good!' she said. 'Good! Good morning, good night, good!'

The unpacking began. 'Kiki was dreadful in the train

home,' said Jack, struggling with an armful of clothes, and dropping half of them. 'She got under the carriage seat to pick over some old toffee papers there, and such a nice old man got in. Kiki stuffed the toffee papers into the turn-ups of his trousers – you should just have seen his face when he bent down and saw them!'

'And then she began to bark like a dog,' said Lucy-Ann with a giggle, 'and the poor old man leapt off his seat as if he'd been shot.'

'Bang-bang,' put in Kiki. 'Pop-pop. Pop goes the weasel. Wipe your feet and shut the door.'

'Oh, Kiki! It's nice to have you again with your silly talk,' said Mrs Cunningham, laughing. Kiki put up her crest and sidled over to her. She rubbed her head against Mrs Cunningham's hand like a cat.

'I always expect you to purr, Kiki, when you do that,' said Mrs Cunningham, scratching the parrot's head.

The unpacking was soon done. It was very simple really. Dirty clothes were pitched into the enormous linen-basket, the rest were pitched into drawers.

'Can't think why people ever make a fuss about packing or unpacking,' said Jack. 'Kiki, take your head out of my pocket. What's this sudden craze for toffees? Do you want to get your beak stuck so that you can't talk?'

Kiki took her head out of Jack's pocket, and screeched triumphantly. She had found a toffee. Now she would have a perfectly lovely time unwrapping the paper, talking to herself all the while.

'Well, that'll keep her quiet for a bit,' said Dinah thankfully. 'Kiki's always so noisy when she's excited.'

'So are you,' said Philip at once. Dinah glared at him.

'Shut up, you two,' said Jack. 'No sparring on the first day of hols. Gosh, look at Lucy-Ann going up the stairs dropping a pair of socks on every step!'

The telephone bell rang. Mrs Cunningham ran to answer it. 'That will be Bill!' she said.

It was. There was a short conversation which consisted mostly of 'Yes. No. I see. I suppose so. No, of course not. Yes. Yes. No, Bill. Right. Yes, I'll explain. See you tonight then. Goodbye.'

'What's he say?' asked Lucy-Ann. 'Is he coming soon? I do want to see him.'

'Yes, he's coming this evening, about half past five,' said Mrs Cunningham. The four children didn't think she looked very pleased. She opened her mouth to say something, hesitated, and then closed it again.

'Mother, what was it you said you'd explain?' said Philip at once. 'We heard you say, "Yes, I'll explain". Was it something you had to tell us? What is it?'

'Don't say it's anything horrid,' said Lucy-Ann. 'Bill *is* coming away with us, isn't he?'

'Oh yes,' said Mrs Cunningham. 'Well – I hope you won't mind, my dears – but he badly wants us to take someone else with us.'

'Who?' asked everyone at once, and they all looked so fierce that Mrs Cunningham was quite surprised.

'Not his old aunt?' said Dinah. 'Oh, Mother, don't say it's someone we've got to be on our best behaviour with all the time.'

'No, of course not,' said her mother. 'It's a small boy – the nephew of a friend of Bill's.'

'Do we know him? What's his name?' asked Jack.

'Bill didn't tell me his name,' said Mrs Cunningham.

'Why can't he go to his own home for the holidays?' asked Dinah in disgust. 'I don't like small boys. Why should *we* have to have him? He'll probably spoil everything for us!'

'Oh no he won't,' said Philip, at once. 'Small boys have to toe the line with us, don't they, Jack? We get enough of them and their fatheadedness at school – *we* know how to deal with them all right.'

'Yes, but why has he got to come to *us?*' persisted Dinah. 'Hasn't he got a home?'

'Oh yes – but he's a foreigner,' said her mother. 'He's been sent to school in England to have a good English education. I should imagine his family want him to have a few weeks in a British family now, and experience a little of our homelife. Also, I gather there is some difficulty at his home at the moment – illness, I should think.'

'Oh well – we'll have to make the best of it,' said Lucy-Ann, picturing a very little, homesick boy, and thinking that she would comfort him and make a fuss of him.

'We'll park him with you then, Lucy-Ann,' said Dinah, who didn't like small boys at all, or small girls either. 'You can wheel him about in a pram and put him to bed at night!'

'Don't be silly, Dinah. He won't be as small as that!' said her mother. 'Now – have you finished? It's almost lunchtime, so go and wash your hands and brush your hair.'

'Wash your hands, brush your hair, wipe your feet, blow your nose,' shouted Kiki. 'Brush your hands, blow your feet, wipe your – your – your . . .'

'Yes – you've got a bit muddled, old thing,' said Jack with a laugh. Kiki flew to his shoulder, and began to pull at Jack's ear lovingly. Then, as she heard the sound of the gong suddenly booming out, she gave a loud screech and flew into the dining room. She knew what *that* sound meant!

'Jack! Kiki will peck all the tomatoes if you don't keep an eye on her,' called Mrs Cunningham. 'Go after her, quickly!'

But there was no need to say that – everyone had rushed to the dining room at the first sound of the gong!

Enid Blyton

The Adventure series

The Island of ADVENTURE
Enid Blyton
"I loved this series as a child"
Cressida Cowell

The Castle of ADVENTURE
Enid Blyton
"I loved this series as a child"
Cressida Cowell

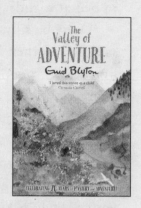

The Valley of ADVENTURE
Enid Blyton
"I loved this series as a child"
Cressida Cowell

The Sea of ADVENTURE
Enid Blyton
"I loved this series as a child"
Cressida Cowell

Which ones have you read?

The Mountain of ADVENTURE
Enid Blyton
"I loved this series as a child"
Cressida Cowell

The Ship of ADVENTURE
Enid Blyton
"I loved this series as a child"
Cressida Cowell

The Circus of ADVENTURE
Enid Blyton
"I loved this series as a child"
Cressida Cowell

The River of ADVENTURE
Enid Blyton
"I loved this series as a child"
Cressida Cowell